The Legend of the Pikesville Cave

by Thomas B. Barker

Copyright © 2016 by Thomas B. Barker

Fifth Printing June, 2016

All right reserved, including the right to reproduce this work in any form whatsoever without permission in writing from the Author, except for brief passages in connection with a review.

ISBN-13: 978-1514721681

ISBN-10: 1514721686

For information write:
Thomas B. Barker
1223 Lake Point Drive
Webster, NY 14580
TBBEQA@MAC.COM
Personal Web: http://tombarker.net

Thomas B. Barker 1941 -

Printed on demand in the United States of America
by Createspace, an Amazon Company

Table of Contents

Chapter   Page

1	The Mercenary from Bavaria	5
2	Military Training Camp	23
3	An Interesting Assignment	39
4	Uncle Al's Potion	47
5	Perfecting The Blast	53
6	Ordinance Takes Over	57
7	The Battle of Pea Ridge	69
8	The Shenandoah Valley and the End of the War	85
9	Scouting The West	117
10	Having a Blast on the Railroad	131
11	Maria	155
12	The Tunnel	173
13	The New Town	187
14	The Magic Elixir	195
15	The Panic of 1873	207
	Epilog	219
	Author's Notes	229
	About the Author	232

Dedication

To the entrepreneurs who made this Country of the United States of America what it is today.

Hurricane!

1861 On a sailing ship in the middle of the Atlantic Ocean heading to the shores of North America.

"Blast you all, ye lubbers! Now lively now. Hang on to those sheets and don't let 'em go loose again like ye jest did. I swear, I'll toss overboard the first lubber who lets go!"

The first mate was furious with the "voluntary" crew of boys who knew nothing about sailing. The regular sailors had been drinking too much and were down below. They were useless and their punishment would be meted out by the captain if the ship ever made it through the hurricane winds they were encountering.

This crew of boys was not trained in sailing and the ropes burned their hands. Even though there were hardly any sails up, the ship was crashing through the waves faster than it had ever done before on this long ocean voyage.

One of the big boys began to slip and as he did, he lost his grip on the rope that the mate called a "sheet." He tried to grab hold again, but he failed. The mate was sure-footed from his years of sailing experience and grabbed the boy by his arm and leg and swung him around and over the rail into the churning sea.

"Told ye I'd throw ye overboard!" chanted the mate.

Despite the sound of the wind, there was utter silence among the remaining ninety-nine boys on that ill-fated ship. Gustave wondered if he would survive this ordeal.

Part 1

Coming to America

Chapter 1
The Mercenary From Bavaria

"Auf Wiedersehen," said Gustave Pikestein to his mother. His eyes were filled with tears. "I don't think I will ever see you again."

He gave her one last hug and boarded the wagon bound for the river boat and the ship that would take him to the war in the New World. The money he received from the recruiter would keep Gretel comfortable for a while at least. His father, Otto had squandered his soldier's earnings on drink, died, and left the family destitute. Their little house in a village in southern Bavaria was all Gustave and his mother had in the world. Gustave was not optimistic about his new "job" as a soldier in the United States of America. At best he would survive the battles and possibly seek his fortune in the land he was headed towards. At worst, he expected to become "cannon fodder" in a bloody battle in a land he knew little about.

The wagon bounced on the rock strewn road. But he was accustomed to this kind of rough ride and some of the pay the recruiter had advanced him jingled in his pocket as the wagon rambled along. "Why not just jump off and skip the voyage across the Atlantic to New York?" he thought as the money tempted him. But this was American money. It could not be spent in any part of Germany or his native Bavaria. Besides, the recruiter would not give his mother's share to her

6 Chapter 1 A Mercenary from Bavaria

until Gustave was on the boat and down the river. That share would be 200 pfennig as agreed when Gustave put his signature on the contract. Gustave was a man of honor (he *was* 17) and would not go back on his contract! The die was cast and he would soon be in America in a training camp learning how to fire rifles or maybe even a cannon, so he thought.

The river boat trip to the ocean port and the sailing ship in which he would cross the Atlantic was far longer than he had expected. *The world is very big*, he thought as the boatman navigated the swirling water and avoided the treacherous rocks, logs, and other boats in their path. *Maybe the American war will be over when I get there*, he mused hoping to avoid conflict and danger. His father had told stories of the battles he was a part of during the frequent wars that raged throughout Europe as one king wanted to overpower another king, not caring about the consequences that befell the population.

Wounded soldiers often returned to their villages with missing arms or legs, if they returned at all. While there was relative peace in this year of 1861, there had been rumors circulating among the elders in the village of a conflict with Prussia over a disagreement on the unification of the Germanic States. Gustave thought he might be better off in the New World conflict than in his native land where his father had fought and died a pauper. Besides, the money the recruiter had promised seemed a good deal for his mother. *Die here or there, what's the difference*, he thought as the boat came to shore for the night.

A New Friend

Besides Gustave, there were three other recruits on board as well as the recruiter who had paid the boatman for this journey. The boys kept pretty much to themselves hunched behind

The Legend of the Pikesville Cave 7

big barrels of wine and packing crates filled with cloth. These items were on their way to the harbor and ships that sailed around the world. Gustave did not know the other boys and did not care to make new friends. They were from other villages along the river and seemed big, rough, and crude - good soldier material but not good friend material. They were also a bit older than Gustave.

At the end of each day, there was often enough time for the recruiter to seek out new candidates in the nearby villages when the boat stopped along the river and tied up to a dock. Today, this busy recruiter picked up a fifth boy. This one was a bit friendlier than the others and seemed to be more like Gustave in stature and age.

"Hello, I'm Gill. What's your name?" he spoke as he approached Gustave with an outstretched hand. Gustave returned the gesture and felt a strong grip from this seemingly small boy. "I'm called Gustave - after my great, great uncle who came from Sweden. My, you have a strong handshake!"

Gill looked Gustave straight in the eye. "You going off soldiering in America?"

"That is what I am intending," replied Gustave. "We can talk about that later, but first come on over here behind this packing crate and have some supper. You must be hungry. I am."

The two boys picked up a bowl of stew that the boatman had prepared and a slice of brown bread that the recruiter

8　　Chapter 1 A Mercenary from Bavaria

had brought in from the village. They sat on a makeshift bench on the stern of the boat near a packing crate. It was just next to the tiller that the boatman skillfully plied against the current and guided the boat down stream.

"Pretty good stew," said Gill. "But not as good as my mother makes."

"It's food anyway and my mother is getting a good deal of money for my soldiering. How about you?"

"My mother is getting 300 Pfennig and I got two gold American coins."

"Three hundred?! My mother only got 200 and I have silver, not gold," replied Gustave feeling cheated.

"What about the other boys on board? How much did they get?" interjected Gill in a consolatory manner.

"I don't know. I haven't talked with them since we began this journey," said Gustave as he soaked up some stew gravy with the dense brown bread.

"I think we should talk to the recruiter about this," said Gill. "All's fair in love and war, after all."

"I don't want to upset him, Gill. Let's leave things alone for now. I've been on this river boat a lot longer than you will be. It is possible that my "pay" is based on how far we need to travel. It costs money to have this boat take us to the harbor. I wonder if the boy who was on the boat when I boarded got a much as I did?" mused Gustave as he finished his supper.

They would be at the harbor tomorrow and the ship would begin the voyage on the outgoing tide the next day. Gustave began to gather his belongings in the sack he had brought

The Legend of the Pikesville Cave

from home. Gill found a spot on the deck to stretch out and sleep. He put his head on his loosely tied sack and watched the sky. The clouds were scuttling past the full moon and the crickets were chirping on the shore.

A Long Ocean Voyage

The harbor was bustling with activity as the boys disembarked from their river boat which was dwarfed by the gigantic ocean ships. The recruiter led them to the ship that would take them to America. There were other recruiters doing the same and there were over 100 young Germanic boys lined up ready to climb the gang plank and their new life (or death) in the "New World." Gustave, Gill, and the other three boys from their river boat were presented to the master of the ship who promptly paid their recruiter some money. Without a word, the recruiter turned away from them and headed back up river, undoubtedly on a quest for more soldier material and probably big profits. Slowly the hundred budding soldiers boarded the ship.

"Come on you lubbers, get aboard. We ain't got all day to mollycoddle the likes of you," shouted the Captain from the foredeck. The boys began to hurry as the crew started to pull in the ropes that held the ship to the dock.

"You there!" shouted one of the crew to Gustave, "Grab this line and pull for all you're worth. Har Har Har." Gustave tried to pull, but the rope was tied fast to the dock. The boat was pulling away and the rope slipped through

10   Chapter 1 A Mercenary from Bavaria

his hands. It was a rough rope and it burned as it grazed his skin. "Ouch!" he cried as the crewman laughed. "Let it go lubber, you fool." Gustave looked at his bloody hand as the rope slowly dragged off the deck and fell limply into the harbor slightly staining the water with his blood. Gill came over to him and wiped the blood off with a rag he had found in a bucket on the deck.

"That'll teach you to think before you act, lubber," laughed the crewman. "Now get you to the doctor. He'll fix you up right good."

Gill and Gustave found a door in the rear of the ship and over the entrance was the sign, 'Doctor.' They knocked and a man opened the door after a few minutes.

"Come right in my boy," said the kindly old man. "The crew always seems to get one of our passengers in trouble at the start of a trip across the ocean. You will be all right." He guided them down a ladder into a big room with a number of hammocks. He said, "Let me get some salve for that rope burn," as he opened a cabinet and extracted a jar of a thick, smelly substance and began to spread it on Gustave's hands. It felt soothing and soon the burn seemed to magically go away. "You will be fit as a fiddle in a few days. But don't go licking this stuff when you eat. Tastes awful! You can rub it in some more until it disappears into your skin. See me tomorrow for another application."

"Thank you, sir," stammered Gustave as he backed away from the doctor and headed up the ladder to the deck.

The ship was heading into the open ocean and as it cleared the outer harbor it began to toss up and down. As the sails filled, the tossing stabilized, but there was still a certain amount of rocking, and the spray from the bow hitting the waves made the deck wet.

The Legend of the Pikesville Cave

The captain stood amidships on a pedestal and bellowed over the sound of the water and wind, "Today we begin our voyage across the Atlantic Ocean. Bein' as it's August, we may hit some heavy weather as we approach the North American continent in early September. But don't you worry none at all, I've made this crossing scores of times and never lost a mate." With that, the captain headed to his cabin leaving the hundred boys with no idea what to do.

"You are off to soldiering like the others we have taken from this God-forsaken country on the last voyage," said a sailor. "I'm first mate and you will follow my orders or, by thunder, I'll toss you overboard!" It was the same sailor who had told Gustave to hold the rope.

"Not a nice man," commented Gill under his breath.

"I don't like him," replied Gustave as he headed to the top of the ladder that was midships and headed down into the interior of the big ship. He and Gill picked up their meager belongings that were still in makeshift sacks on the end of poles. "Where ya go'in?" growled the first mate.

"We thought we would check out our cabins, sir," they replied in unison.

"Cabins?! Har Har. Ye don't deserve cabins, ye scum. Get to the aft deck where the *passenger accommodations* are located and bunk down like the rest of the soldier scum!"

The aft deck was completely empty, except for a few rags and a some barrels of

water that were tied down with heavy ropes. Gill and Gustave followed the rest of the boys and found a little piece of the deck to claim as their own.

"This is going to be a long voyage and I'm already tired of the sea," said Gustave. Gill patted his friend on the shoulder and tried to calm him down. He was just as upset, scared, and sad as his new friend. They sat on the deck and felt the boat rising and falling as the waves crashed all around them. Soon, the rhythm of the boat relaxed their tired bones and their eyes became mesmerized by the shifting horizon. They fell fast asleep.

Gustave's Dream

The bugler's blare woke Gustave with a start. He quickly donned his blue jacket and pants. He ran his fingers through his mussy hair trying to get the snarls out. He pulled on his boots and rubbed the crusty out of his eyes. Gill was doing the same and they almost bumped into each other as they pushed the opening to the tent apart and emerged into the cool morning air. The sun was already up on this early summer day.

"Ready for breakfast?" asked Gill who was always hungry. Gustave replied, "Wonder what Cookie has prepared today?"

They soon smelled bacon and headed in the direction of that wonderful aroma. Softboiled eggs were in a large metal bowl and heaps of corn muffins lay on a platter next to the ham. They grabbed plates and forks from the nearby table. Others in their platoon were slowly assembling with their plates.

"I am going to need 4 eggs this morning," said Gill as he picked the hot, brown eggs up with his fingers. They

The Legend of the Pikesville Cave 13

were a small, specialized platoon and they ate well, for Cookie was good at what he did. In fact all of the members of their platoon did very well at what they did - scouting and infiltrating the enemy. While they wore the Union Blue uniform of the US army, they often donned the gray garb of the Confederacy and snuck behind the lines to see what was going on. Technically, they were spies and would be shot immediately if discovered.

But today was a big day. The lieutenant was planning a significant infiltration into the nearby Confederate camp. That camp was a supply depot and had a rail line running right through it. Gustave's platoon was going to do more than just spy on the enemy. They were going to blow up the train, engine, and all as it entered the camp.

As the early breakfast drew to a close, the lieutenant addressed his eight German privates. He spoke in a broken German tongue but the troops understood him well enough to learn the details of the plan. "Mine herren, ve vilst gaben in ein few minuten, widt da explosives und meeten da train vhen it slows onen da curva."

They headed out along the hidden trail with backpacks filled with explosive. Gustave's pack had the fuses and caps which were kept separate from the actual sticks of explosives for safety.

As they neared the curve and heard the engine struggling against the grade, six of them ran across the track and hid in the trees with rifles ready to distract the engineer and brakeman. Gustave and Gill waited until the distraction was underway and then made the leap to the midsection of the engine where Gill planted the explosives and Gustave expertly placed the blasting caps and fuse. It was a long fuse that was timed to blow the engine as it entered the enemy camp. Gustave lit the fuse and jumped from the engine into the bushes.

The camp was not far from where the explosive had been attached to the engine and, as it slowed to a halt in the middle of the camp, a roaring explosion blew a hole in the side of the boiler.

Steam and engine parts were scattered all over the camp. The cars containing the supplies were immediately blazing and the ammunition in one of the cars blew to high heaven.

Gustave and Gill rejoined the rest of their platoon and hightailed it back to their own lines. There was so much confusion at the confederate camp that they had no problem making their escape. But, as Gustave was just about clear, he felt a stabbing sensation in his side. Was it a bayonet from the enemy?

"Wake up!" It was the First Mate kicking Gustave in the side with his pointed boot. "Swab the deck with the rest of the scum!" shouted the First Mate. There were buckets of water with mops sticking up from them. Gustave was feeling a bit queasy from the tossing ship, but he did not want to get thrown overboard as the First Mate had threatened, so he grabbed a mop and began to mop the deck. The handle was rough on his injured hands, but he kept going. Gill was also doing this chore. Many of the other boys were hanging over the side of the ship. Gustave could not see any land and the sea looked dark and gray with heavy clouds on the horizon. He felt a trickle of rain against his

The Legend of the Pikesville Cave 15

cheek. Soon the swabbing of the deck was finished and the boys who were not hanging over the side of the ship assembled on the foredeck for orders.

"Ye know now that ye are not passengers on this fine ship," said the First Mate. "Ye are our cargo. Don't ye forget it. But ye needs to eat and there's grub down below. Now, get to it and then back on deck with the likes of ye."

Gustave was hoping for a fine breakfast like he had dreamed about. But the food was a thin porridge that was plopped into a tin cup. There wasn't even a spoon and he had to drink the tasteless semi liquid.

A rough looking sailor with a peg leg mumbled under his breath, "Keep yer cups, me buck-os. That's what ye will be using on the 'tire crossing and iffen ye lose it, you get nothing to eats. I'm the cook and I makes yer grub - so like it or lump it!"

Gustave and Gill finished their breakfast, returned to the aft deck, and shoved their cups with their stuff in their little cloth sacks. Gustave's hands were raw from the deck-mopping that had made the rope burns from last night sting and burn. He headed to the doctor's cabin.

The kindly doctor was giving "one of the lads" a concoction for his upset stomach. "Here ya be, my friend. Drink this down and stay on deck. Breathe in the fresh sea air and you will be OK by super time." The big bruiser of a boy walked past Gustave and Gill and looked a bit under the weather. He did not make the usual threatening gestures to either of them as he and his friends had done when they all boarded the ship only a day ago.

"The sea always breaks the rough ones with its ups and downs. Now let's get more ointment for your rope burns. Made you swab the deck, did he? He's a nasty one, that

16   Chapter 1 A Mercenary from Bavaria

First Mate," said the doctor as he rubbed more of the magic lotion into Gustave's hands. It worked it's miracle again.

"Now you can supplement the cook's food with some of the apples and lemons I have down here. Citrus is important for a long sea voyage. You wouldn't want to get scurvy now, would ya?" said the doctor as he reached into barrel and produced a red apple for each of them. They enjoyed their fruit and threw the cores (what little that was left of them) into the ocean that was speeding by with big, frothy waves.

"I wonder what time it is?" inquired Gill. Just then they heard the ship's bell. Ding-Ding. Ding-Ding. A sailor was standing idly by the rail. He looked somewhat friendly which was unusual for a sailor, so they asked him about the time and what the bells meant.

"Pretty simple, mates. The day is set up in 6 watches of 4 hours each. We begin with one bell at the start of each watch cycle. So this morning, at 8:30 we had one bell. You just heard four bells and each additional bell adds a half hour to the time. So it's now 10:00 and since the sun is out, it's morning. Next time we hear four bells, it will be 2:00 in the afternoon. My next watch is at five bells. What time would that be?"

Gustave thought for a moment. He was good at counting."That would be 10:30," he reasoned.

"Right on me bucko! So, I'm going up to the wheel, which is my post, for the next 4 hours. You are welcome to watch with me."

Gill and Gustave followed the helmsman to the wheel. They observed as the watch changed. The gimbaled compass rocked gently in its housing.

Gustave asked, "Why are we heading Northward?" The sailor replied, "We are tacking, me bucko. We have to head

The Legend of the Pikesville Cave 17

off the wind to get where we are going. The wind would be right in our teeth if we headed due west. That would put us in irons and stop the boat in its tracks. So we head about 45 degrees off the wind, Northwest and then we tack 45 degrees off the wind to the Southwest. It's a tedious process, but we make progress. Half of my watch is on this tack and the ship will turn southward at eight bells. Watch the lads then as they trim the sails for the southwest tack. They're like monkeys in the rigging!"

Gustave and Gill were fascinated by the precision of the ship's operation. The wheel seemed to be straining with every wave and the helmsman had it lashed to ease the effort on his part.

Ding-Ding. Ding-Ding. Ding-Ding. Ding-Ding. The ship's bell sang out and the helmsman unlashed the wheel and began to spin it. As he did so, the ship turned into the wind and the crew tended the sails so they were now on the opposite tack from the previous settings. The rigging strained against the tremendous pressure of the wind and the masts groaned and creaked. But soon all was smooth again and the ship was crashing through the waves in a graceful rhythm.

It was dinner time and the boys all stood in line for what turned out to be a bit of a better meal than breakfast. There was bread and cheese and the doctor had another apple for those who wanted one. The bread was still warm from the ship's gimbaled oven.

~~~~~~~~~~

While time seemed to pass very slowly, Gustave and Gill soon got into the ship's rhythm, which was both ex-

18   Chapter 1 A Mercenary from Bavaria

citing and full of good lessons. While the other boys just grumbled about the food, the work, and the weather, Gill and Gustave, the two smallest of this cargo of the hundred mercenaries, stuck it out and bettered themselves from the experience. They learned about ropes and knots, navigation and weather, and especially how to survive in trying situations like the hurricane that occurred while they were about halfway across the ocean.

Gustave grimaced as he remembered the sight of the boy being tossed overboard. He and Gill had survived that storm because they had learned more about sailing than the rest of the boys. Their ship was sturdy and there were only a few splintered poles and torn sails. The drunken sailors who had figuratively abandoned ship and were down below during the hurricane were punished and their pay was docked. They were now busy mending the sails and repairing the broken wood.

The nightmare was over but one of the boys was no longer with them. It must have been a terrible death, but being shot by a musket bullet or worse – by a cannon ball – was probably no better. After all, they were going to be soldiers.

~~~~~~~~

At last the Captain appeared on deck. He had been below deck for most of the voyage. When he was seen on deck, he appeared a bit unstable as if drunk. Rumor among the crew was that he had a lot of grog in his cabin and drank all day long.

It was up to the nasty First Mate to run the ship which he did with an iron hand. Gustave was wary of the First Mate's tricks and careful not to get another rope burn like he got on that first day. The doctor's salve healed the soreness and soon Gustave was doing many sailor duties with excellent skill. This made him special with the First Mate who softened toward his first victim.

But now it was the Captain stood on the foredeck and pointed toward the bow of the ship. "We're nearly finished with this crossing. I see the land birds in our wake. Soon we'll hear the cry, ***Land Ho***."

As if by magic the Captain's words were made to ring true. Just after two bells on that brisk early September morning, the lookout in the crows nest made the testament to the sighting of land.

"Good to be in sight of land. The apple barrel is nearly empty," reported the Doctor as he headed down to his cabin and 'hospital.' The fairly big space was empty. The other boys seemed to have gotten their sea legs after a few days and did not need his ministering for most parts of the voyage. There were, of course, the usual scrapes and bruises when the ship lurched and an unsteady boy fell to the deck. "But no major damage," the doctor put it as he expertly applied salve or lotion to the injury.

The sailor that Gill and Gustave had befriended stood watch at the wheel on the day they came in sight of land. "We won't be in port for a couple of days. We're a bit south of New York and will be *reaching* north. You'll like that point of the sail. We are 90 degrees to the wind and sometimes we can nearly run on a very *broad reach* with the wind almost on our backs. Fastest point of sail, me bucks."

The ship slowly headed north until they were a few miles off the coast. It began to tear through the waves and seemed to fly as they began to sail on a broad reach. Our two industrious boys filed that bit of knowledge into their brains and enjoyed the ride to their ultimate destination.

Now, the ship was quite stable and running smooth and flat. The cook had slaughtered one of the little pigs that had been eating corn in the hold. He built a big cooking fire that was roaring on the deck in a metal tub raised from the wooden planks with heavy metal rods that were affixed to large logs for stability. The pig was on a spit, sizzling with succulent juices.

"Our Captain always has a big meal on the last night of our crossing," said the doctor who had come up from below. "He can afford it. He'll sell you 100 mercenaries for $300 a head, plus the cargo below will bring a tidy profit for him. He owns this ship and he does not have to share any of this loot with an owner like other Captains."

Those words tumbled over in Gustave's mind. Had he made a mistake in signing on with the recruiter back home? He wondered how much a dollar was worth in his home country's money. He had two of the dollar coins in his pocket and his mother had received 200 Pfennig. The Captain had paid the recruiter some money. Who was ahead in this deal?

"It's ironic that you boys are essentially being sold into military slavery. The war that is being fought in the United States is about slavery and the Union is on the side of freedom," mused the Doctor. "This ship was once a black slaver, just a few years ago. That is what the Captain meant

The Legend of the Pikesville Cave 21

when he said he had made this crossing scores of times before. Only back then he made landfall in the Southern States. Ports like Savannah. He didn't have the guaranteed $300 a head, but had to rely on supply and demand. Some black slaves only fetched a few dollars at auction. He's getting his money from rich citizens who don't want to fight for their country. There are lot of them in New York City. Eat well, boys. Tomorrow, you are off to war."

Land at Last

The ship docked on a crowded wharf. The boys gathered their belongings and walked the plank down to the solid ground. Gustave felt a bit unsteady, as if the ground was rocking under his feet. "Feel a bit like the ship is still under you, me bucko?" asked the friendly sailor who had taught them all about ropes, knots, navigation, and weather.

"Yes, I do, sir," replied Gustave.

"It's normal. You body still thinks it's on the ship. You'll get over it in a few days. Now, be safe in your new adventures," and he headed down the road. He had been at the wheel during the storm and had a pocket full of his pay. His pay had not been docked as the drunken sailors. Those sailors were lucky to not have been up on charges and a jail sentence for their dereliction of duty. They had been made to work twice as hard and for one third their pay as punishment.

All the boys were huddled in an area just across from the ship. The First Mate and the Captain were arguing with a man in a top hat. They could barely hear the conversation and it was in rapid English. Some of the words stood out like, "Two hundred" and "all I can pay." The Captain looked disappointed. The First Mate was angry and struck the man on the jaw as he walked away. His top hat fell off into the mud in the road. "We'll find a better deal for the full $300 a head as we expected," said the hotheaded First Mate.

The Captain picked up the hat and brushed it off as he handed it to the man. "Give me $275 and we'll call it a deal," he said. The top hat man replied, "$250 and keep that hothead away from me." The man in the top hat and the Captain shook hands.

The next thing Gustave knew, there was a string of wagons drawing up to the boys' location and they all began to board. There were planks to sit on and there were two soldiers with muskets on each wagon as well as the driver. There were ten boys to a wagon. Gill and Gustave were in the third wagon. They left the wharf and headed toward the countryside.

Chapter 2
Military Training Camp

Gustave and Gill bounced along the dirt road in the military wagon on their way to a camp somewhere along a river. The other eight German recruits in their wagon complained about the rough ride.

"They just grumble all the time," observed Gill.

Gustave replied under his breath, "I wonder what kind of soldiers they are going to make? I learned from my father that fighting was not a pleasant occupation, and it took a lot of fortitude to survive the hazards of battle, or even just waiting for the fight. My father said, 'waiting was the worst part of soldiering.'"

Just then, the wagon train came to a halt and they were ordered out. The uncomfortable wagon ride was not so long after all.

A three car troop train was waiting along the side of the dirt road. They scrambled into the cars and took their seats. This was a lot more comfortable than the hard planked seats of the wagons. These cars had padded seats, a smooth ride, and was much faster than the wagons. None of the

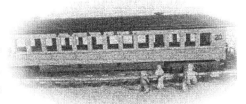

24   Chapter 2 Military Training Camp

German recruits could speak English and they had no idea where they were going. But there was one phrase they kept hearing over and over again, "Old Fort Schuyler."

One of the officers in Gill and Gustave's car began to speak in German. "Welcome to the United States of America. You now are members of the Union Army. Your rank at this point is only recruits, or as we call you *Fresh Fish*. You will earn your private stripe when you complete basic training. I am sergeant Benedict Berger, your drill master. After your three weeks of training, we will join General Franz Sigel in Missouri, which is farther west. Your basic training is at Old Fort Schuyler near Utica, New York. This train is taking us there and we should arrive before nightfall. A hot meal will be ready for you in camp and we will show you how to set you up your tents where you will sleep. Now, rest up. Tomorrow is the first day of some rugged work!"

"He sounds like a good fellow and I like the fact that I can understand him," said Gustave as he stretched out on the seat and dozed off. Gill did the same and soon both were sleeping soundly to the smooth rhythm of the rocking train.

Gill's Dream

The night air swirled the fallen leaves and made a rustling sound. The full moon made the thin clouds glow, but there was not enough light to cast shadows and their dark clothes helped blend them in with the trees and the tall grass. There was no trail, but the enemy camp was not so far away that they could not miss their goal. Gustav had the blasting caps and Gill had the explosives and fuses. They were a team and had been on many such missions. The plan was to plant the explosives, set and light the

The Legend of the Pikesville Cave   25

fuses, and then make a hasty exit as quietly as possible. The ammunition dump would explode, depriving the Confederates of the weapons they sorely needed for the battle that would rage the next day. Gill and Gustave had been trained especially for this type of operation because of their small size, speed, and agility. Now they were slithering on their bellies toward the ammo. It was heavily guarded, but they had eluded guards before and silently made their way to the main tent. Gustave placed the fuse in the cap and shoved it into one of the 10 sticks of explosive. They were using a slow burning fuse which Gill lit with a match drawn from his tinder box. Just then, the moon broke through the light cloud cover and their escape was hampered by sudden visibility.

The guards saw movement in the grass and shouted, "Halt, who goes there?!" There was an explosion and a screeching noise like a musket ball flying over Gill's head.

~~~~~~~

Gill was jolted awake by his friend's shaking and the sound of the train's brakes. "We're in camp, Gill. Wake up!"

With a groggy look on his face, Gill said, "I've just had the most frightening dream. You and I were blowing up an enemy ammunition dump. We almost got away with it, but the moon came out and the guards saw our motion in the tall grass. I thought I heard a musket ball sail over my head, but you woke me. Thanks for saving me from that dream."

"Funny, Gill, I had a dream about blowing up a train the first night on the ship. I wonder if we are really going to do that?"

26 Chapter 2 Military Training Camp

The train was slowing as it pulled into Utica. "We must have slept a long time," remarked Gustave as he looked out the window. It was dark, but there were flickering specks of light in the distance.

Sergeant Berger roused the recruits and had them line up on the small station platform. They were a gangly bunch and some were still groggy from their naps. They swayed back and forth, still experiencing the sea voyage.

"Stand up straight! Get in line!" shouted the sergeant. "Now march like soldiers," he continued.

A couple of the more awkward boys tripped on their feet and fell to the ground. As they did, they almost toppled Gustave and Gill who kept marching. The downed boys caught up and began again with a bit more steadiness. As they reached the outskirts of the camp where the specks of light had been seen from the train station, Gustave began to smell the aroma of food. He was hungry.

Camp Schuyler and Food

The aroma of food filled the hungry boys' nostrils as they came into the camp. They hadn't had a decent meal since the pig roast on the ship that had brought them to the shores of the United States. They had munched on some hard, brown bread on the train, but it was dry and tasteless.

"We pitch the tents first. Then we can eat," boomed sergeant Berger. The recruits were led to a big tent where there were piles of canvas, ropes, and stakes. "Find three other recruits and pick up the tent parts from the quartermaster. There will be four sleeping in each tent," Berger continued.

Gill and Gustave looked for two other boys, but they were the last two. Since there were thirty all together in their

The Legend of the Pikesville Cave 27

squad, there had to be one tent with only two occupants. The quartermaster handed Gill and Gustave a smaller canvas package. It was their two man tent and they were glad not to be bunking with those other boys.

Gill was quite good at pitching the tent. "I did a lot of camping back home," he said as he showed Gustave how to pound the stakes at an angle with the hammer they were given. Soon their tent was erected and they had shelter. The tent would provide some protection from the cool September night air and any rain that may fall. The other boys had difficulty with their tents and sergeant Berger was frustrated with their efforts. "No food until you get those tents up," he bellowed. "You two seem to know a bit about tents. Go help the others," continued Berger in a much lower tone. Gill and Gustave went over to help their clumsy fellow recruits. Everyone was hungry and the sooner the tents were up, the sooner they would eat.

The camp was not a pretty sight. Some of the tents were lopsided and others were neither snug nor straight. Sergeant Berger looked at the uneven camp.

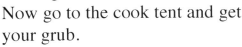

"Good enough for now. I never thought I would have to teach you how to pitch a tent. But we'll add that as part of your basic training. Now go to the cook tent and get your grub.
IN AN ORDERLY FASHION!"

28   Chapter 2 Military Training Camp

Fearing the wrath of the sergeant, the boys walked in a dejected gait to the wonderful smells emanating from the pots near the center of the camp. They found metal plates and spoons.

"Line up here and we'll put your stew on your plate. You get a chunk of bread and a mug of coffee. Tonight we have an apple for everyone also," said the cook as he began to ladle the hot meal on the plates. The boys accepted the food and sat down on benches at a table. After wolfing down the stew, they wiped their plates with the fresh bread, not missing one drop of the tasty gravy.

When they were finished they went over to a trough of water and washed their plates as they had been shown by the cook's assistant, who rewarded them with an apple. Not many of the German boys had coffee that night. Beer was their usual drink back in the Fatherland. Coffee seemed bitter and almost tasteless. Gustave did try the coffee and found that with a little bit of sugar, it was just OK but not his favorite drink.

Little campfires dotted the campground and soldiers with muskets stood guard. This was the first time the recruits had a break from the travel and they felt good about solid ground and the lack of motion. They still had their "sailor legs" and were not quite over their long sea voyage. Yet, they joked about what was to come the next day and the next weeks.

~~~~~~~~

The bugler's horn woke the "fresh fish" from their dreams. Sergeant Berger called the boys to assemble in front of their tents. There was a chill in the early-morning air of late September. The sun was just on the horizon. The smell of food was drifting throughout the camp. "Come on, we've got a

The Legend of the Pikesville Cave 29

war to fight!" shouted the sergeant. "Over to the supply tent. Today you are issued uniforms and your weapon."

They marched in a groggy formation to the quartermaster's tent. The quartermaster spoke German and they understood his instructions. There they found clothing and boots to fit each of them and a rifled musket with an ammunition belt. They also were given a square bag made of cloth with a long strap.

"That's your haversack. You put your personal items and your food in it, along with your cooking utensils. No more mess tent when you are on maneuvers," said the quartermaster. Each recruit got a plate, a cup, a spoon and a fork, and a drawstring bag to hold them snug.

The musket they picked up was a Springfield 1861. The 1861 was a muzzle loading weapon that could hit and kill at 300 yards and weighed 9 pounds (or so said the quartermaster). "Your sergeant will teach you how to load, aim and fire this fine musket," continued the quartermaster. "He is an excellent marksman himself and can hit a cork off a bottle at 100 yards. You should aim for that kind of precision."

The gun was heavy on their shoulders and the ammunition belt felt tight as it hung on their bellies. "OK, you "fish," off to your tents, stow your gear and suit up in your uniforms. Then to the mess tent for breakfast," ordered the Sergeant.

Breakfast was not as tasty as the stew they had had the night before. It was a simple porridge with a lump of brown sugar. But it was hot and filled the void in their stomachs. Soon breakfast was over and they were again called to attention by the drill sergeant.

30   Chapter 2 Military Training Camp

"Now line up. Each tent of four "fish" will form a row. No, not like that - across in a row!" bellowed sergeant Berger.

The recruits soon learned how to make a formation. Each tent of four boys, spread out across on the parade ground assigned to their squad of thirty. Then the next tent's occupants lined up in a row one arm length behind the first tent's occupants, and so on, until seven rows formed a column. Gill and Gustave, being only a tent of two, lined up at the end of the column as the eighth row. They made a neat centered row with one "fish" to the left in front of Gill and one 'fish' to the right in front of Gustave. Sergeant Berger nodded approval.

"Now we begin the drill," he said. "Begin with your left foot. Then your right. So, left, right, left. Left, right, left. Left, right, left. Left, right, left."

But soon the "fresh fish" were out of step and the sergeant cried out, "Halt! Let's try it again." And so they tried and tried all morning long. By the time noon rolled around, there was a sorry bunch of "fresh fish" on the parade ground.

"Achtung!" shouted Berger. "We eat dinner now and will continue all afternoon with this until you get it right." Everybody was tired including the sergeant. "My feet ache," said Gustave. "Mine too," echoed Gill. They lined up at the mess tent and produced their plates and cups. They were served baked beans with huge lumps of salt pork. Most drank water, but Gustave tried coffee again with a bit more sugar. The taste of coffee was growing on him and the buzz kept him sharp and awake. The others were dozing off after the rigorous morning of drilling, and the heavy dinner.

But they all were back at it after only an hour of rest. "Left, right, left. Left, right, left. Left, right, left. Left, right, left. **All together now**," bellowed Berger.

The Legend of the Pikesville Cave

Then the entire squad began together, "Left, right, left. Left, right, left. Left, right, left. Left, right. left."

By mid afternoon, the fish were doing a respectable march and it was time to begin the real maneuvers, for they were running out of parade ground!

"Left, right, HALT!" commanded the sergeant. "Now we will learn how to come about in formation. When I say 'Right Face,' you will turn to your right. When I say, 'About Face,' you will turn in the other direction."

It was a comedy of errors on the right face. Half of the troops turned to their left and crashed into the *fish* who was next to him. "Don't you know right from left? Try it again," said the sergeant. This time only a few turned the wrong way. "Try it again," said the sergeant. This time only two turned the wrong way. "Try it again. RIGHT Face," said the sergeant. This time nobody turned the wrong way and they continued marching. Now they were marching in formation, making a large clockwise circle in a much bigger part of the parade ground.

By the time supper time came around, the fish were exhausted, sweaty, and ready for a good night's sleep. Supper was potatoes and beef, but this time not in a stew, The potatoes were boiled and the beef was roasted and cut off a shank that was suspended over a fire of glowing embers.

Most of the camp was asleep before the sun had relinquished its last crimson glow. The night air was cool and the fish curled up in the stout wool blankets that were a part of their basic camp gear. The larger training camp tents were snug and if rain should come, the trench they had dug around the tent would keep the water from flooding the floor, which was made of a tarred canvas.

32   Chapter 2 Military Training Camp

~~~~~~~

The second morning was much the same as the first. The bugle woke them early and the breakfast was the same porridge with brown sugar. Coffee was becoming more the favored beverage by many of the troops (as they began to call themselves).

The drill was relentless. It started at sunrise, continued until dinner time at noon and only ended at supper time. New routines were added, with "about face" and "left face" completing the catalog of commands. Of course, "halt" and "at ease" were two of the favorites of the troops.

On the fifth day the sergeant felt that the fish were ready to drill with their weapons, ammunition belts, and haversacks.

"Today we begin weapons training," announced Berger. "This morning, we will march with our full combat equipment. So, get your muskets, ammunition belts, and haversacks. On the double!"

The boys ran to their tents and retrieved their muskets, ammunition belts, and haversacks. The haversacks were mostly empty, but not for long. The sergeant directed them to the quartermaster tent where they were each given a square of canvas about six foot on each side. There were buttons on one side and buttonholes on the other side. "Each one of you will get half a tent. Pair up and practice making your shelter just as when we camp on maneuvers," said the quartermaster.

"You can use your muskets to make the tent poles. Place your bayonets on the firing end of the musket and plunge it into the ground. String the heavy rope between two muskets to support the top and connect the two halves of the canvas to form the sides of the tent," continued the quartermaster.

The Legend of the Pikesville Cave   33

Now all the members of sergeant Berger's squad were in tents of two. Gill and Gustave were already paired up and were quick to follow the tent construction instructions. "It's not very big," said Gill.

"Not much bigger than a tent for a dog," quipped Gustave.

"Hope we fit." Gill then coined the name. "It's a dog tent!" And he began to yelp like a dog. As the other fledgling soldiers completed their tent construction, they all chimed in. "Arff-arff, woff-woff, **g r o w l**."

"Quiet, you pups!" cautioned sergeant Berger as he came to inspect the new encampment. "That's not a worthy use of a fine weapon. Who told you to use your muskets and bayonets like that?"

One of the bigger boys replied, "**Sir**, the quartermaster, **sir**."

"Oh, he did, did he? I'll have to see about this misuse of weaponry." And he stormed off to the supply tent.

Soon he returned with a less than happy expression on his face. "The higher ups have sanctioned this use of the muskets for the dog tents (as you call them). Who am I, just a drill sergeant, to question the mighty generals? But by thunder, we'll just have to make sure your muskets are fit for their intended use. Take your tents down now, stow your gear and get ready for a march with full haversacks, muskets, and ammunition belts."

"**Sir**, We need a marching song, **Sir**." sang out Gustave.

The big sergeant listened to Gustave with a sympathetic smile on his face. "Do you have a suggestion?"

"**Sir**, We will be fighting for General Sigel, **sir**, so let's sing his troops' song, **sir**. **Sir**, I heard it from one of the other squads who was singing it as they marched yesterday, **sir**."

"Can you tells us the words?" questioned Berger.

"**Sir**, it goes something like this, **sir**:

*I've come shust now to tells you how
I goes mit regimentals,
To Schlauch dem voes of Liberty,
Like dem ole Continentals
Vot fights mit England, long ago,
To save de Yankee Eagle;
Und now I gets mine sojer clothes,
I'm going to fight mit Sigel.
Ya! Das ist drue, I shpeaks mit you,
I'm going to fight mit Sigel.*

The sergeant addressed his fish, "I know this song. We have sung it in marches out in Missouri. It has some English words in it and some mixed words. You need to learn English, which is the official language of this United States. So, we'll start with this first verse and the chorus. Nothing like a lively marching song to relieve the tedium of marching drills!"

And so the *Berger Squad* began the first of many fully equipped drills that morning in mid September in Utica New York. While the drilling was tiring, the song raised the spirits of the fish and soon they became men of action. Berger added more words to the song and by late September they had the entire song committed to memory, and at the same time they were learning English.

The Legend of the Pikesville Cave

Ven I comes from de Deutch Countree,
I vorks somedimes at baking;
Den I keeps a lager bier saloon,
Und den I goes shoemaking;
But now I was a sojer been
To save de Yankee Eagle;
To Schlauch dem tam Secession volks,
I'm going to fight mit Sigel.
Ya! Das ist drue, I shpeaks mit you,
I'm going to fight mit Sigel.

I gets ein tam big rifle guns,
Und puts him to mine shoulder,
Den march so bold, like a big jack-horse,
Und may been someding bolder;
I goes off mit de volunteers,
To save de Yankee Eagle;
To give dem Rebel vellers fits,
I'm going to fight mit Sigel.
Ya! Das ist drue, I shpeaks mit you,
I'm going to fight mit Sigel.

Dem Deutshen mens mit Sigel's band,
At fighting have no rival;
Un ven Cheff Davis' mens we meet,
Ve Schlauch em like de tuyvil;
Dere's only one ting vot I fear,
Ven pattling for de Eagle;
I vont get not no lager bier,
Ven I goes to fight mit Sigel.
Ya! Das ist drue, I shpeaks mit you,
I'm going to fight mit Sigel.

As the days passed by quickly, the men were shown how to clean and oil their muskets. Each ammunition belt held a cartridge box with "40 dead men," as they called the

40 rounds of 58 caliber Minié balls. There were powder and percussion caps, and the men learned how to load the powder from the small paper container, ram the Minié ball with the ram rod, place the cap, aim, and fire. The two flip up sights were set either for the long distances of 500 yards or 300 yards. With both sights down, the aim was for the more likely 100 yard distance that would be involved in most of the combat from the front lines of battle.

~~~~~~~~

On the last day of training camp, all three squads from the ship were assembled on the parade ground. A captain from Missouri had arrived the night before on the troop train that awaited now in the Utica Station. It would transport the fresh recruits out to Missouri and the captain was now in command of these privates.

But before the men headed off to the train for the three day trip out west, they were ready to show their new commander what they were made of.

Each squad sergeant paraded his newly trained troops to the assigned position of the parade ground. They were fully equipped and ready to show how they would behave in battle.

The first squad to show their skills, lined up as a combat column. Their muskets were brought to the ready and they quickly loaded and fired on the bales of hay set 300 yards on the other side of the field. There were paper representations of enemy soldiers attached to the hay bales. After firing from the front of the formation and the subsequent three rows, there was nothing left of the paper enemy. The newly minted soldiers were firing at a rate of three rounds a minute per man.

The Legend of the Pikesville Cave

"Excellent!" exclaimed the captain.

The next squad had 40 recruits and was the largest of the three trained that September. They also got an *excellent* from the captain.

Now it was Gustave and Gill's squad of 30 recruits. Gill was especially accurate in his aim and Gustave was not far behind in his ability to pick off small objects at even 300 yards. The four deep column fired at the newly placed paper enemy at 300 yards. Not only did the paper enemy disappear in less than a minute of rapid fire, but the haystacks disintegrated in a cloud of dust!

Now it was the marksmen's turn. Full bottles of wine had been securely placed into holders attached to the tops of poles. The corks were withdrawn to just about the point where the cork would go "pop" when pulled. Gill was first. His musket was already loaded and he took careful aim. The first bottle of wine popped opened as the Minié ball hit the cork! But his was not just a display of aiming skill. He had his musket loaded again and the second bottle of wine was opened. Before you could say, "Cock Robin" the third bottle was uncorked and ready to drink. But this was not the end. Gustave aimed his musket at the fourth bottle and uncorked it immediately after the first three were opened. His musket was loaded and again another bottle was opened, followed by the 6th bottle. The captain was using his watch to time this incredible display of shooting.

"They have done this wine bottle opening in less than a minute!" he exclaimed. "Fantastic performance. I have brought citations from headquarters for all of you newly minted privates for your excellent shooting. And for the two precision marksmen, I am personally granting an *on the field promotion* to corporal. Congratulations to all of you and welcome to General Sigel's brigade. Now let's drink the wine that has been so skillfully opened for us!"

It was a time for celebration at Fort Schuyler. More wine was uncorked (but by more conventional methods) and all the newly minted privates and two corporals had a good taste of the fine French wine. The camp staff had a bit more wine as well as the captain from HQ in Missouri. They all sang the Sigel's brigade song and ate the best meal they could remember, with pumpkin pie for dessert.

But as the sun began to set, the festivities came to a close and the troops began their march down to the train station where the troop train was up to steam and ready to take them to their new camp in the west.

Gustave and Gill were invited to sit with captain Morgan and he revealed his plans for the newly promoted corporals. His proposal was interesting and exciting. Something they had dreamed about.

Chapter 3
An Interesting
Assignment

Gustave and Gill continued in the troop train listening to Captain Morgan tell his ideas about a unique task for both of them in a special platoon headed by a Lieutenant Chester.

"General Sigel and his staff always need information on enemy troop size, location, and supply lines before a battle. Lieutenant Chester's small platoon is one of those intelligence gathering outfits. I am always on the alert to find potential members of his platoon," said the captain in a hushed tone of voice. "You two seem to fit the mold. Your size and agility are exactly what we need. You seem to learn fast and execute with excellent ability."

"What is involved in learning this new skill, **sir**?" inquired Gustave.

"You will join Lieutenant Chester's platoon on my recommendation. He is short two men because of an illness called the *flux* that seems to be running through the camp in Missouri."

"Yes, we have heard of the *flux*, but nobody in our squad ever got it. It's a nasty sickness that keeps a soldier in the latrine all the time," interjected Gill. He continued, "We boil all our drinking water before we put it in our canteens and hope that will keep the *flux* out. Our sanitary advisor told us about that trick."

"Good for you men. That's what I mean about you being quick studies and smart soldiers. You have even more

40 Chapter 3 An Interesting Assignment

made my decision a solid choice to place you in Lieutenant Chester's platoon and your field promotion," continued the captain.

They sat in silence for a number of minutes contemplating the conversation that just ensued. Gustave broke the silence first. "How dangerous is the information gathering job?"

The captain replied, "Sometimes you will be behind enemy lines and in disguise. That is a very dangerous activity if you are caught - especially if the disguise is a Confederate uniform. You would be shot as a spy!"

"I guess the idea is NOT to get caught," interjected Gill with a bit of humor in his voice.

"Right, that's why you will need special training. Lieutenant Chester has perfected a number of maneuvers to avoid detection and methods to get back to our lines safely," assured the captain. "We can talk more about this and some of the other covert activities in his platoon. He reports directly to me and I convey the intelligence you will gather directly to the general and his staff. But now let's settle down and get some sleep. It's getting late and we still have two days of train travel before we reach General Sigel's main camp."

The entire troop car was filled with blue uniformed soldiers falling asleep as the train headed west.

~~~~~~~

As morning broke, there was a light autumn rain washing the windows of the troop train cars. There was no bugler on the train, but there was a cook in the baggage car and he was clanging his big spoon on a large pot. Gus-

The Legend of the Pikesville Cave 41

tave awoke with a start. He rubbed his eyes and straightened up. Gill and the captain were doing the same. There was a general sound of groaning as the rest of the troops awoke.

Gustave's back ached and his legs were stiff. He felt a tingling in one of his hands that had been tucked in a crack of the seat cushion. He shook it and the tingling subsided.

"It appears that cookie has a breakfast ready for us. He is a good cook and it sure beats eating skillygalee like we do when going into battle in the field," laughed the captain.

"What's skillygalee?" asked Gill trying to pronounce the new English word correctly.

"Why it's a concoction you cook up with hardtack and pork fat. You know, hardtack, that tooth-dullers bread. Crumble it up and add it to the hot bacon fat and you have a reasonable ration any time of the day. That's what is called skillygalee. I've eaten it on the battlefield and survived," explained the captain. "But now let's indulge in a real breakfast!"

They filed to the baggage car in an orderly manner. The cook had set up a kitchen in one corner of the swaying car and was cooking a breakfast of oatmeal, bacon and eggs, and corn bread. Each soldier heaped his plate with the fine food and carefully headed back to the seat in the car he had slept in the night before. They were getting accustomed to the swaying train and nothing was spilled as they made their way back.

"Stay here, corporals," said the captain. "We can continue our conversation more in private at this small table."

Gill and Gustave sat down at the small table for four and the cook joined them. "Great meal, cookie," complimented the captain.

42 Chapter 3 An Interesting Assignment

"Wait till you see what's for dinner and supper today," commented the cook. He was a jolly fellow who looked like he enjoyed his cooking. He had a round belly and a smile that ran from one side of his face to the other. "An army runs on its stomach and I feed that army," he said proudly.

"Cookie has been with General Sigel for many years," remarked the captain.

"Why, I knew the general long before he got his promotion in August. We're old buddies and he is the best. You know his orders are written in both English and German so you krauts can understand them," boasted the cook.

"Cookie, I think that promotion to brigadier was a wise decision by President Lincoln. Sigel has a huge influence on German immigrants who abhor slavery. He has recruited many of these fellows to his ranks. Oh, by the way, these two fellows are becoming quite fluent in English. They won't need those German language orders," added the captain.

They finished their breakfast and left their plates and forks in the tub next to the cook stove. An orderly who worked with the cook began to clean up the dishes. He had some soap which made the chore easy.

"Got any more of that soap, private?" asked the captain. "We sure could use it if we ever find a river that is warm enough to take a bath in it."

The orderly reached into a bin and produced a cake of soap. This was a precious commodity in the time of war and the captain thanked him profusely.

"We got to take a bath back at training camp once on our only day off," remarked Gill. "The river we found was cold, but it felt good to wash our hair which had become

The Legend of the Pikesville Cave 43

so matted down, we didn't ever need to comb it! Would have been great if we had some soap back then."

They walked back to their car and sat down. The captain pulled out a cigar. "Want a smoke?"

"No thanks sir, we don't indulge," replied Gill.

The captain drew them closer and in a hushed voice told them the next part of their new assignment. "Besides spying, you will also engage in demolition and general nuisance against the enemy."

"You mean blowing up things?" asked Gustave.

"Exactly, my boy," replied the Captain.

"We learned about blasting powder in training camp," added Gill. "It seemed dangerous - carrying the blasting powder, and it takes a lot to do much damage," he added. "There should be a better way to do things like that."

The captain added, "There is a new, very powerful explosive. But it is *so* explosive that if you shake it even a little bit, it explodes. So, it's impossible to transport it, which makes it impractical."

"I know," interjected Gill. "My father was working with my uncle Al and that's how my father died. He was trying to move a very small amount of this liquid explosive from a workbench and he dropped it. The whole room was destroyed. That's why I am here. I might have continued my father's work with Uncle Al, but I decided to come to America and seek my fortune."

"Gill, we've been friends now for some months and you never told me your story," Gustave said in a sad tone.

"I guess I wanted to keep it a family secret. My Uncle Al was furious about the destroyed building and felt that his brother had sabotaged his work. I was told to leave and never come back. I found the work interesting, but I

44   Chapter 3 An Interesting Assignment

was not welcome any more. That's why I never told you or anyone about this terrible experience," said Gill reluctantly.

Both the captain and Gustave remained silent for many minutes out of respect for the tragedy that had befallen Gill. When they resumed their conversation, they were less enthusiastic about blowing up things.

~~~~~~~

It was nearly evening as the troop train pulled into the station which was their final destination. The three day journey was over and they were in a very large Union camp. It must have been ten times the size of Old Fort Schuyler.

Part 2

Booming Times

Chapter 4
Uncle Al's Potion

Gill and Gustave alighted from the train with their gear and headed to the Headquarters tent. The captain led the troops and showed them where to go.

"Gill, Gustave, follow me. The rest of you are assigned to Company G. Go to that tent and see the sergeant who speaks German and he can get you signed up," said the captain in German.

"This way to Company MI-5, the intelligence force that I command," said the captain as he strode across the paths in the busy encampment with Gustave and Gill right behind him.

They entered a large tent that had roped off sections with makeshift desks made out of planks mounted on bricks. There were canvas chairs at the desks and rows of cots with blankets neatly folded on them.

"You two are to be assigned to Platoon SD under Lieutenant Chester over in the back of the tent on the left. First we need to get you into this army officially. The administrative sergeant will help you fill out the paperwork and get you into the payroll system. Yes, you get paid for your services," continued the captain in a very officious manner.

They walked over to the sergeant's desk and reported for duty. The sergeant had already been informed by the captain about the new recruits to Company MI-5 and had the paperwork started. "Just sign your name on this paper, and you will be on the payroll. You get $13 a month as corporals," announced the sergeant. They dutifully affixed

48   Chapter 4 Uncle Al's Potion

their signatures on the form and stepped back for more instructions.

"Your platoon is back there. All of the men are out right now, so pick a bunk that is not occupied and put your gear on the cot. I'm not busy now, so come back here and I'll show you where the rest of the platoon is training," advised the sergeant as he went back to filing their sign up forms.

They wandered back to the bunk area and found two cots that were unoccupied and put their stuff down. Then they went back to the sergeant's desk, where he got up and motioned for them to follow him outside the tent.

There was a faint chill in the late September air here in Missouri. A squad was marching by and singing the Sigel song.

Ya! Das ist drue, I shpeaks mit you,
I'm going to fight mit Sigel.

The squad faded off in the distance as the sergeant walked briskly toward a cordoned off section of the encampment where there were half a dozen enlisted men and a lieutenant gathered around a barrel. They were being very careful with something. As Gustave and Gill drew closer, they saw the reason for the caution. The barrel was marked with the word, **EXPLOSIVES**.

"Here is your platoon," said the sergeant. "Lieutenant Chester, here are the new recruits to your platoon,

The Legend of the Pikesville Cave

49

Corporals Gustave Pikestein and Gilbert Nobel. Hand-picked by the captain."

"Welcome to the SD," the lieutenant extended his hand in greeting. "We are small, but very effective at what we do. Right now we are testing various charges of blasting powder. This we obtained from ordinance, but we are attempting to make our own blasting chemicals. I understand corporal Gilbert has had some experience in Europe with explosives."

"Yes, **sir**, I have, **sir**," saluted Gill. "And please call me Gill, **sir**."

"No need for all that kind of military formality here, Gill. We work as a tight-knit team and sometimes we need to act quickly. So dispense with the **sir**. I want to hear more about your experience. Please share your knowledge with all of us."

Gill told the story of how he had worked with his father's brother in a city in Sweden that was just across the sea from his home in Germany. He explained how he had seen a new type of explosive that was so powerful that just a small bottle blew up an entire house.

"Your story is amazing, Gill. I heard of this nitroglycerine at West Point when we were studying explosives. Its major problem, as you have pointed out with the unfortunate death of your father, is how volatile it is and how it can't be transported without extreme care. We used small drops of nitroglycerine in chemistry class to see its potential. I blew up an entire brick structure with my drop. I wish there were a way to handle it safely and use it instead of blasting powder. It takes so much blasting powder to do the same job as just a few drops of nitro."

The lieutenant waited for a reply from Gill after his long speech. Gill replied, "I think uncle Al was looking

50   Chapter 4 Uncle Al's Potion

for ways to keep the nitro from bumping into itself in its bottle. He was soaking sawdust with nitroglycerine and adding a small amount of another chemical (I can't think of its name, something like soda or the like) to buffer (he said) the reaction."

"Humm.... soda ash?" interjected the lieutenant.

"No, something like sodium carb..."

"Sodium carbonate!" exclaimed the lieutenant. "We learned how to make sodium carbonate from bicarbonate of soda - or baking soda. The cooks use baking soda to make biscuits. If we just heat it at 200 degrees, in an hour we have sodium carbonate! That's an easy ingredient to obtain from the cooks. Sawdust is also easy and we have a small quantity of nitro. Let's try to make uncle Al's potion!"

~~~~~~~~

It was late that afternoon when the platoon made the first trial of "Uncle Al's Blaster Stick." They had produced some sodium carbonate from sodium bicarbonate they obtained from the cook. With two man crosscut saws, they made a lot of sawdust. Gill thought that the formula he had seen being made at his uncle's factory used about 3 times the amount of nitroglycerine as the sawdust and the sodium carbonate was added like salt to a potato. They first mixed the sawdust and sodium carbonate. Then they poured the mixture into a paper cylinder. The paper was a heavy type and had been coated with wax on the inside and outside. Then, they carefully poured the nitro into the cylinder. The liquid quickly was absorbed by the sawdust mixture. "Now, how do we set it off?" was the question on everyone's mind.

The Legend of the Pikesville Cave   51

"How about using some ordinary gun powder attached to a fuse?" suggested one of the platoon members. All of these soldiers were sharp characters with a lot of experience. Gill and Gustave liked them for their innovative nature and spontaneous ideas like this one.

Again, some wax was heated and coated on a small paper tube. Gunpowder was inserted into this paper tube that was open on one end. A small amount of wax was formed around a fuse with the short end of the fuse extending into the open end of the tube so it was touching the gun powder. A thin seal was placed on the open end of the paper tube to keep the gunpowder from falling out. The fuse/igniter was designed to fit into the nitro cylinder.

"Ready to test this new explosive?" asked the lieutenant. "Gill, you do the honors."

Gill slid the explosive stick into a hole that had been drilled into a dead tree stump. The fuse was three feet long and it had about two feet exposed outside the hole. The blasting stick was well into the base of the tree stump. Gill lit a match and touched it to the fuse - and then ran like the devil was chasing him. The fuse burned slowly but soon came to the opening and the glow disappeared down the hole.

All at once, there was a tremendous explosion. The tree stump was hurdled skyward and a cloud of dust surrounded the spot where it had been. Bits of wood from the stump rained down on the field.

"We did it!" was the proud exclamation of the eight platoon members and their leader, all in unison. They had worked as a team, bringing all the components together.

Lieutenant Chester shook the hands of each man and patted Gill on the back. "Good work, men. We have a very promising new explosive with which to thwart the enemy. Now let's go to supper and thank the cook for his contribution with the ingredient he supplied."

They walked off the field as the other soldiers looked in awe at what they had accomplished in a single day. Captain Morgan sat with them at supper and listened to their tale of the invention of the new explosive.

Chapter 5
Perfecting The Blast

The next day turned out to be rainy. While other soldiers drilled in the rain, platoon SD remained in the tent. They were documenting their efforts of the previous day.

"At West Point we learned in chemistry class to make detailed reports on our experiments," stated Lieutenant Chester. "We also need to think of other experiments to perfect the blast stick."

They began a list of things to test and wrote them on a large sheet of paper mounted on a board that was attached to a makeshift stand.

Hans was first to contribute, "Can we transport the blast stick safely?"

"How fine should the sawdust be?" interjected Rupert.

Jerry added, "How much sodium carbonate do we need? Where do we get more? The cook is practically out of baking soda!"

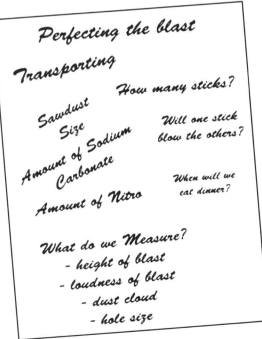

Perfecting the blast
Transporting
Sawdust
Size
Amount of Sodium Carbonate
Amount of Nitro
How many sticks?
Will one stick blow the others?
When will we eat dinner?
What do we Measure?
- height of blast
- loudness of blast
- dust cloud
- hole size

54   Chapter 5 Perfecting the Blast

"And where do we get the nitro and how much of that do we need per stick?" questioned Cliff.

"Slow down men, I can't write that fast," cautioned the lieutenant. "And what will we measure as a result of these changes to the blast stick formulation?"

The troop members slowed down and then in rapid fire began to suggest things to measure like blast height and loudness, hole size and dust cloud.

"I wonder if one stick is enough and can we use multiple sticks and does one fuse blow up the whole pack of sticks?" mused Gustave excitedly.

It must have been getting near the noon hour for there was an under someone's breath mumble, "When do we eat dinner?"

"OK, break for dinner and then back to writing the report," commanded Lieutenant Chester. "We need to get our report to Captain Morgan by supper time. He will need to approve the supplies and we'll have to coordinate with ordinance. They will be making the explosives."

The group broke for dinner, which was their favorite: baked beans with plenty of salt pork and fresh bread and just-churned butter. They ate a hearty meal and then went back to their tent while the other troops drilled in the heavy rain.

The lieutenant sat at the makeshift desk and began to write to report on the new blast stick. As he wrote, he asked the members of his platoon for information and clarification. Indeed, they were a good team. After a while the questions and clarifications subsided. Lieutenant Chester continued to write the report. At that point the one sergeant in the platoon began. "Besides the new blast stick, we need to perfect our sneaking around skills. Gill and Gustave, have either of you ever been trained or involved in spying techniques?"

The Legend of the Pikesville Cave   55

Gustave spoke for them, "No, we were trained only in marching and firing muskets."

"Just as I thought. None of us are given that kind of specialized training during the basics. Our platoon has been working on those methods for some time, but have not put them into practice **yet**," the sergeant replied. "Here is the basic idea. Rupert, Jerry, Stephen, Alexander, Joseph chime in if I forget some of the things we have been working on. As we approach enemy camps, we first watch for the routine: when the guards change; when the meals are served; when they drill. Did I miss anything?"

Jerry interjected, "When they sleep."

"Yes, of course. That's when the camp is most vulnerable," said Sergeant Cliff.

The rain was easing as Cliff continued with his instructions which included the use of spy scopes, clothing that was specially made to blend in with the surrounding countryside, and belly crawling in tall grass. "Now that we seem to have a safe, powerful explosive, we will begin combining our undetected observation skills and enemy camp infiltration with the planting of the blast sticks in the enemy's ammunition dumps, destroying troop trains, and other nuisances that will give them setbacks," continued the sergeant.

"The *blast report* is finished," interrupted the lieutenant. "I'll get it off to the captain and then rejoin you to formulate our next plans."

It was getting late in the day and the sun was low on the horizon behind some broken clouds that were chasing the rain away. The eight members of SD platoon sat and thought about their role in this war that had begun only a few months ago. Most of the citizens (especially in the

North) believed the war was nothing much and would be over in less than a year. Those in command knew differently. The South or Confederate States had almost as many West Point trained officers as the North or as they called themselves, The Union. There were many soldiers who believed in their cause, volunteered for duty, and were ready to fight to the death to defend their side's honor. Neither Gustave nor Gill had this motivation. But they were both committed to fighting and they were glad to be doing that fighting *mit Sigel.*

~~~~~~~~

Shortly the lieutenant returned. "You all look so pensive," he observed. "What's going on?"

"I think the men are tired after all our planning and thinking," suggested Sergeant Cliff, speaking for his men.

Gill piped in, "It seems like such a big job for only nine of us including the lieutenant. I, for one, am a bit apprehensive about the danger. What if we are caught spying?"

"Spies are shot," cautioned the lieutenant. "That's why we will drill constantly on our techniques and *not* get caught. But *our* danger is actually less than being in the front lines of battle."

Chapter 6
Ordinance Takes Over

While the rest of the troops tried to dry out from the drenching rain of the previous day, the members of platoon SD were dry in their section of the large tent they and other specialized units and platoons were assigned. Among those specialty units was the Quartermaster Corps, which worked closely with "The Sanitary," whose job it was primarily to provide healthy food to and see to the general health of the soldiers in a camp. Historically, in war, there was more death due to sickness than the actual battle. Some estimates of non-combat deaths in European conflicts reached five times combat deaths. The Sanitary was organized to reduce such five to one ratios. The Union was serious about keeping their soldiers alive before, during, and after combat. This was a departure from other wars and how soldiers were treated in other countries.

Besides Quartermaster and Sanitary, the others in the big tent were cooks (although their time was mostly spent in the cook tent), ordinance, strategy, and intelligence. Keeping the related activities in one place helped coordinate battle plans and there was a large area set aside to accommodate joint meetings among the officers of the companies. Platoon SD was a part of the military intelligence company commanded by Captain Morgan.

This morning, Captain Morgan was meeting with Captain Schultz of ordinance to discuss the blast sticks. Lieutenant

58 Chapter 6 Ordinance Takes Over

Chester accompanied Morgan to the meeting. Schultz had his Lieutenant Gruber, a chemist by training, at his side.

The members of platoon SD watched from afar as the meeting progressed through the morning. Gustave and Gill sat on two of the makeshift chairs con-structed of bales of hay that dotted the tent. Their sergeant had decided to skip drill that morning just in case the meeting needed inputs from him or the cor-porals. The others were sit-ting around and convers-ing at low tones.

"Gill, tell me more about your family and how you decided to join the Ameri-can war," began Gustave.

"Only if you tell me about your family too," replied Gill. "You first."

"OK," said Gustave. "Here goes. My father was a sol-dier and he was pretty good at it. There always seemed to be wars going on so he never was 'out of work' as many of the men in our village were. He met my mother when he was a little older than I am now - I think he was about nineteen. His soldiering had taken him to the Baltic Sea on the tip of Germany. It was not a long journey to Ger-many from Sweden and many Swedish women had made the crossing because they had heard the army was near and they were that kind of women who 'followed the army.' I guess my father and mother hit it off almost immediately and when he came home to Bavaria during a short peri-

The Legend of the Pikesville Cave 59

od of peace he brought her with him. My older sister was born a few weeks later. Afterwards they were married in the Catholic Church in Munich. With his army pay, he was able to buy a small cottage and the little family seemed to prosper. However there was not much work for a soldier in our tiny village, which was far from the capital. Soon my father had to go off to war again. I was born on February 20, 1844, during my father's fighting in the Schleswig War in Denmark. Later, he returned to our village and we lived carefully off his pay for a number of years.

"As I got older, I began to do chores. When I was nine, I brought home some money, as did my sister. My father did very little and drank more and more. He said he was a 'broken man' due to his fighting, and while he was not wounded, he had seen so many of his fellow soldiers wounded, dismembered, or killed, he never wanted to go off soldiering again. He often would tell war stories at the local tavern for free drinks. He died when I was fourteen.

My sister was seventeen when she left home and my mother and I have not heard back from her since. When *I* turned seventeen the next year, I decided to try my hand at soldiering since it seemed to run in my family - my grandfather was killed in a war long before I ever knew him. So, Gill, *we* met on the river boat and crossed the ocean together and now find ourselves here. I think my father never got beyond a private, so I've achieved the highest rank in my family. Now what about you?"

Gill began, "Now my mother is German and my father is Swedish. Just the opposite of you."

Lieutenant Chester approached the two boys, "Gill, we need you in the meeting."

"I'll continue this later, Gustave," said Gill as he rose to walk off with the lieutenant.

60   Chapter 6 Ordinance Takes Over

They went to the meeting area, where the lieutenant introduced Gill to the others. Captain Morgan added his embellishment to the introduction, "Besides bringing us the formula for the blast sticks, Corporal Nobel is one of the best sharpshooters I have ever had the pleasure to watch demonstrate his skills. He shot the corks out of three wine bottles at 400 yards [an exaggeration of course] in less than three minutes!"

"Yes, yes, Morgan. You can curb your enthusiasm. Let's get to the problem at hand now," interrupted Captain Schultz of ordinance. "We need to know if our knowledge of this new way to handle nitro is widely circulated, especially in Europe, where our enemy might get wind of it an then use it against us."

Captain Morgan pointed to Gill and asked, "Gill, what do you know about the blast sticks as far as who knows about them and if they are being used in Europe?"

"**Sir**, I know that my uncle Al was a stickler for secrecy. I would not have learned about them if I had not been working in his development laboratories. My father was his brother and I helped my father with his work which involved trying out different absorbent materials - like the sawdust we used in our successful implementation of the blast stick. As far as I know, only a handful of people know how to make a blast stick. Uncle Al is working on a patent and will set it forth when he finds the best way to make the explosive. I would say he is a few years away from the patent, based on how long it took him to get where he was a year ago which was when I saw him last."

"That's good," replied Schultz. "Now we need to continue your uncle's work here in the Union. My company will supply the raw materials and the personnel to do the

The Legend of the Pikesville Cave

testing with the cooperation of the Quartermaster Corps. Your SD platoon will work closely with us since you will be our customers. We want this secret weapon fully field tested and ready to go for some battles that are planned for late winter and early spring next year. I won't tell General Sigel about the blast stick until it is proven for effectiveness, safety, and availability."

The meeting ended and the assignments were in the hands of the platoon lieutenants. One of these assignments was to build a manufacturing laboratory in a very remote part of the camp where nitroglycerine would be produced in sufficient quantity to supply the blast stick experiments. A lab was set up since nitro was almost impossible to transport.

~~~~~~~

While the plan was being implemented, the SD platoon worked on its infiltration drills. Gustave and Gill soon caught on to the art of disguise and learned how to blend in with the scenery. They learned that their camouflage depended on the season with whites for winter, greens for summer and spring and reddish colors for fall. Of course, this also depended on the part of the country they were spying in. Soon the platoon had an extensive array of clothing for any type of situation and they learned how to move in the environment without attracting attention. Usually it was slow and careful movement that worked best.

Their drills were set with half of the platoon doing the sneaking (they were called the "sneakers") while the other half tried to detect them (they were called the "seekers"). This was especially challenging for the sneakers since the detectors were aware of what they were looking for. There

62 Chapter 6 Ordinance Takes Over

were very few opportunities for the members of the SD platoon to kick back and relax as they trained for the big offensive planned for March.

~~~~~~~

Ordinance company worked tirelessly on making nitro-glycerine in their remote laboratory. They did so with no loss of life and with great success in making sufficient quantities to begin the experiments to make according to the plan, "safe to carry and highly explosive blast sticks" by early December. However, they ran into one slight problem. Nitroglycerine freezes at 50 degrees F. With the coming of the cold winter months, the nitro they produced would not flow and mix with the sawdust.

To alleviate this problem a special blast stick fabricating house was built. One room of the building had a Franklin stove, and a good supply of firewood was stored in a shed right outside that room. One of the privates in the SD Platoon was assigned to keep the stove hot all the time, 24 hours a day. The heat from the stove room as it was called was then pumped into the other room of the building. That room was kept at 60 degrees F and it was large enough to store various particle sizes of sawdust and just enough nitro to make up the experimental blast sticks.

Besides the nitro and sawdust, the building which they called among themselves *Blast Central Fabrication* had supplies of wax, paper tubes, and sodium carbonate. The wax was melted on a small stove in a part of the room far away from the nitro.

The ordinance chemists were trained by Lieutenant Swartz, who had also just graduated from West Point in

The Legend of the Pikesville Cave

Lieutenant Chester's class and was well versed in organic chemistry. The two lieutenants often compared notes and exchanged ideas as the work progressed. Their captains praised the cooperation between the ordinance and spy/destruction (SD) platoons.

Again, a large sheet of paper was set on a stand and the experiment was put into a detailed plan of action. The blast sticks that were produced for this experimental plan were stored in another building and labeled according to the identification number in the experimental plan.

Blast Stick Experiment

#	Size	Sawdust	Sod. Carb	Nitro	Response
1	5	Fine 1	0.1	3	
2	10	Fine 1	0.1	3	
3	5	Coarse 1	0.1	3	
4	10	Coarse 1	0.1	3	
5	5	Fine 1	0.4	3	
6	10	Fine 1	0.4	3	
7	5	Coarse 1	0.4	3	
8	10	Coarse 1	0.4	3	
9	5	Fine 2	0.1	4	
10	10	Fine 2	0.1	4	
11	5	Coarse 2	0.1	4	
12	10	Coarse 2	0.1	4	
13	5	Fine 2	0.4	4	
14	10	Fine 2	0.4	4	
15	5	Coarse 2	0.4	4	
16	10	Coarse 2	0.4	4	

Now it was platoon SD's job to test the 16 sticks. Actually there were 32 sticks, since half of the tests involved safety and the other half involved blast effectiveness.

64 Chapter 6 Ordinance Takes Over

The safety tests began first. These involved only the sticks and the blasting caps did not need to be involved since the blast sticks would be carried without the caps inserted. To do this test, the platoon had a member who had the longest throw. Trials were initiated with dummy sticks and Stephen was chosen since he could throw a stick 75 yards which was at least 25 yards longer than anyone else.

The results clearly showed the fine sawdust was the safest in an amazing way. Even at the 75 yard throw the fine sawdust did not blow up when they hit the ground. The coarse sawdust constructed blast sticks all exploded on impact.

Blast Stick Experiment

#	Size	Sawdust	Sod. Carb	Nitro	Response
1	5	Fine 1	0.1	3	No Blow
2	10	Fine 1	0.1	3	No Blow
3	5	Coarse 1	0.1	3	Blow
4	10	Coarse 1	0.1	3	Blow
5	5	Fine 1	0.4	3	No Blow
6	10	Fine 1	0.4	3	No Blow
7	5	Coarse 1	0.4	3	Blow
8	10	Coarse 1	0.4	3	Blow
9	5	Fine 2	0.1	4	No Blow
10	10	Fine 2	0.1	4	No Blow
11	5	Coarse 2	0.1	4	Blow
12	10	Coarse 2	0.1	4	Blow
13	5	Fine 2	0.4	4	No Blow
14	10	Fine 2	0.4	4	No Blow
15	5	Coarse 2	0.4	4	Blow
16	10	Coarse 2	0.4	4	Blow

Lieutenant Chester speculated that the fine material was better able to absorb more of the nitro per volume of total

The Legend of the Pikesville Cave 65

material and therefore was able to withstand the impact better. He said that it is always better to have a rational explanation of an effect in an experiment than to just do what the data says. "Knowing why something happens is always good. It may lead to even better designs. If fine sawdust is good, something even finer that absorbs more may be even better."

But of course, the next test was to see if the fine sawdust blast sticks would explode with a blasting cap and provide the explosive power that was needed.

Blast Stick Experiment

#	Size	Sawdust	Sod. Carb	Nitro	Response
1	5	Fine 1	0.1	3	20 ft high 30 in
2	10	Fine 1	0.1	3	50 ft high 50 in
5	5	Fine 1	0.4	3	Dud
6	10	Fine 1	0.4	3	Dud
9	5	Fine 2	0.1	4	Dud
10	10	Fine 2	0.1	4	Dud
13	5	Fine 2	0.4	4	Dud
14	10	Fine 2	0.4	4	Dud

The blasting caps/fuses were affixed to the remaining 8 experimental blasting sticks and each 5 inch stick was placed in a 12 inch hole in the ground next to a tree stump. The 10 inch sticks were placed in 18 inch holes. The fuses

66   *Chapter 6 Ordinance Takes Over*

were lit one at a time and the result was observed. Only sticks 1 and 2 blew up. The remainder were duds.

Again, lieutenant Chester speculated on the reasons for this event. "It looks like the original formula that Gill brought back from Sweden with the small amount of the sodium carbonate and the ratio of three nitro to one sawdust is the one that works. The ten inch stick has twice the power of the five incher and that makes sense - there's more nitro in it. It looks like we have a safe, powerful design for our new blasting sticks!"

That night there was much celebrating among the platoons that had participated in the experiment. The cook had prepared a special supper with roasted beef and gravy on mashed potatoes with squash. For dessert they had a creamy pudding.

General Sigel joined them and toasted their success with fine German wine which was opened in the conventional manner, and not with gunshots!

Part 3

Combat

Chapter 7
The Battle of Pea Ridge

Winter set in with a vengeance in late December and continued through January and February. Snow covered the ground and it was hard trudging from one part of the camp to the other. The blast stick building was the warmest on the grounds and there were many volunteers who, if they were privileged to know about it, would have liked to serve there despite the danger of the nitro. But it was a secret project now, and SD Platoon and Ordinance were the only "eyes" in *eyes only* protocol.

Ordinance had built up a good supply of the blast sticks and stocked them in another hastily constructed building on the other side of the encampment as far from the production facility as possible.

Christmas came and went. Many of the soldiers were given a short leave to visit their relatives who lived nearby. Gustave and Gill had no relatives in the New Country and just stayed in camp with the other German mercenaries who had come with them on the boat and from other parts of their fatherland. While most of the German immigrants practiced the Lutheran religion, Gustave was from Bavaria, which was Catholic. The Christmas service was Lutheran and Gustave found it not much different from what he remembered of the services in his home village.

70   Chapter 6 The Battle of Pea Ridge

Christmas dinner was roasted turkey and dressing, mashed potatoes, gravy, and winter squash. Pumpkin pie was dessert. Sigel was able to keep his troops fed well despite the corruption that was rampant in the military supply chain.

There was a rumor in the camp about an offensive being planned. The artillery platoons were drilling constantly. Platoon SD was working on winter camouflage and they found tunneling through deep snow was far easier than through the grass. Grass moved, but snow was far more stable and their movements were imperceptible. The *sneakers* were not detected by the *seekers* very often. They were drilling with packs loaded with dummy blast sticks and detonators as well as their muskets and haversacks. It was cumbersome with all that stuff and Gill questioned the wisdom in carrying a big load. Lieutenant Chester explained, "When we do our scouting, we will be out for days getting to the enemy camp. We need our haversacks to carry enough food and ammunition. Our muskets will be needed for defense if we are spotted by an enemy scout. Yes, they have scouts too. Of course, we want to spot the enemy scouts first and cut them down if it does not spoil our cover. And then there is the possibility that the fuse could come loose and we would have to detonate the blast sticks with a well aimed musket ball."

They had practiced detonating blast sticks that were bundled in groups of 5 by hitting the center stick with a Minié ball from their muskets. Gill and Gustave were the best at this because of their fantastic marksmanship. They were designated as "Plan B" if the fuses failed to detonate the blast sticks. Plan B was not the favored detonation approach since it would give away the location of the shooter and the attack would not be much of a surprise.

The Legend of the Pikesville Cave 71

~~~~~~

It was late February and the captain called a conference of his platoons. SD was represented by Lieutenant Chester who, after his briefing came right back to his men.

"This is it. We head out tomorrow. The plan is to drive the enemy further south and keep them out of Missouri forever. Our job is to pinpoint exactly where the enemy is located in Arkansas. General Sigel will lead the First and Second Divisions and General Curtis will lead the Third and Fourth Divisions. Now pack up your haversacks, ready your muskets, and bring enough blast sticks and detonators to blow a supply train if we spot one."

Just as in his dream, Gustave was put in charge of the detonators. He carefully packed them in his *blast bag,* which was a canvas backpack. The other seven men packed their *blast bags* with ten blast sticks each. They had enough explosives to blow up a good part of an ammunition train. None of the men slept well that night because of fright and excitement.

They were up before dawn and ready for the march into Arkansas. The ground was frozen, but there was not much snow and they made good time. Now they were in the forest and had good cover. The map showed the state line about a day's march away. By noon they were about half way, according to the lieutenant's reckoning.

"Break for dinner," he said as they entered a small clearing. "Each team of two can build a small fire and you can fry up your salt pork. Crumble in some hardtack and make yourself a batch of that delicious skillygalee. This is the last time we can cook anything over a fire, so eat heartily."

Gustave made an extra amount of skillygalee and packed it away for supper that night.

"What are you making so much for? Is it that good?" asked Gill.

"I thought we might be hungry at supper time. Skillygalee beats plain *sheet iron crackers* any time," counseled Gustave.

"Good idea, I'll make an extra batch too," chimed in Gill.

Dinner break was too short, but the men knew what they had to do and got on to marching the last miles in good form. As they reached the state line, they could see the glow of campfires in the distance on a low, rolling hill. They also saw a railroad track just ahead. It was dusk at 6 PM.

"Make camp here in the woods," ordered the lieutenant in almost a whisper. "Quiet is the order of the day now. You know the drill. We run silent and we run deep into the enemy territory."

They stowed their packs and muskets. The little two man tents were erected with each of the men of a pair contributing one side. Their muskets became the tent poles. Gill and Gustave crawled into their tent and fell asleep quickly because of the exhausting day of marching. The army issue wool blankets that were in their haversacks kept them insulated from the cold ground. They had pitched their tent on some soft moss and it was not bad for winter camping.

Two of the platoon members were assigned to sentry duty and the lieutenant used their tent in their absence. The sentry shift was set for two hours, so by three AM all four pairs had participated in watching and listening for any sign of trouble.

The Legend of the Pikesville Cave 73

~~~~~~~

Gustave and Gill had the last watch and they carefully woke the others when their watch was over. It was dark, but their eyes had become acclimated and they could see enough to pack up and begin their scouting. They left their heavy haversacks in a secure hiding place that they could find later. They were fully armed with muskets, ammunition belts, and of course the blast sticks in their backpacks. They began the scouting formation, which was purposely broken up into individual teams of two to make a smaller target for probing eyes. They left their camp at five minute intervals and headed in slightly different directions, but always toward the enemy encampment. They had agreed on a password if they should meet in the underbrush. They came up with "Salt Horse" which is the nickname for salt pork which they had for dinner the previous day.

Gill and Gustave headed out and skirted along the railroad track which was leading directly into the Confederate camp. Now they could see artillery parked near the sleeping camp. They counted the cannons and made note of the size of the force. They were surprised by the lack of sentries. The other three small squads of scouts also made estimates of the enemy strength by counting the rows of tents.

Gustave and Gill heard a low rustling to their rear and froze in their tracks. If that sound was being made by an enemy scout, they had to pick him off without a ruckus. A knife would be the weapon of choice in this case. The rustling was still muffled - a sure sign of a trained scout. It was getting closer to their position. They crouched down and drew their

74   Chapter 6 The Battle of Pea Ridge

sharp knives. Gustave was ready to pounce on the now visible moving figure when they heard "Salt Horse!" The password!

It was the lieutenant. He spoke in a low whisper. "We have a demolition job. The ammunition for their artillery is on the train down the tracks about a mile away. We need to sneak there, plant the charges, and then get away. We can't use fuses for this caper since we would be exposed and unable to get away fast enough. We need to use Plan B. That's you two and me. Are you ready to do it?"

"Yes sir," was their enthusiastic response, although they kept their voices down, knowing that any sound above a whisper would be detected by the enemy. The plan was simple. The blast sticks would be planted on the forest side of the ammo cars, out of sight of the camp. Each car of the three car train would need ten blast sticks bundled together and attached to the bottom of the car, with enough of the bundle to be seen by a sharpshooter from the edge of the woods. Gustave, Gill, and the lieutenant would be the sharpshooters and would be positioned at that critical spot. The other three small squads would plant the blast sticks, then return to the woods, and hightail it back to the place they had stored the haversacks, and then head back to the Union camp in a quick march. When the sun rose and there was enough light to get a bead on the blast sticks, Gustave and Gill and the lieutenant would fire their muskets and set off the explosion. Then they would do their own hightailing into the woods and follow the rest of the platoon back to Missouri. Of course there was much danger in this plan. The Confederates would immediately send troops to the woods, and while they would have a head start, there was still a good chance of being caught. Everything they had learned about scouting would be needed to elude the enemy.

The Legend of the Pikesville Cave

~~~~~~~

It was four o'clock in the morning and the plan was about to be executed. The three small squads of two men each made their way in the most stealthy manner possible toward the train. Gustave, Gill, and the lieutenant watched their progress from the edge of the woods. The half moon was behind the thin clouds and this gave the squads just enough light to see what they were doing, but not so much light that they could be detected. It took them over twenty minutes to traverse the distance on their bellies. As they approached the cars of the train, the lieutenant who had field glasses trained on the train and the surrounding area saw some movement from the Confederate side. There *were* sentries! AND they were changing the guard at that very moment. Lieutenant Chester let out a low, but audible signal. "WHO-WHO," came the sound of an owl from his throat. This was the danger signal that they had agreed upon before setting off. The squads immediately froze in place and remained there for many minutes, not moving a muscle.

Then the new set of Confederate sentries stacked their muskets, curled up on the ground, and went to sleep.

"What a bunch of lazy sentries," whispered the lieutenant. "I would have them court-martialed for such behavior. I think this will be an easy war to win."

He gave the all clear signal, "WHO-WHO-WHO." The squads began to move very slowly and approached the sides of the train cars. The idea was to plant the bundle of five blast sticks in the slats of the cars with just enough showing to enable Gustave, Gill, and lieutenant Chester to shoot the center stick of each bundle which would detonate the entire five. All three shots would be fired at once so the entire train of three cars would blow at the same time.

The sticks were planted and the squads began their stealthy withdrawal back to the tree line. It again took them twenty minutes to accomplish this. It was now nearly five AM. "We may as well rest now," said the lieutenant. "Sunrise is not for a couple of hours and the light will be just right at about 7:30. I'll take the first watch."

Gill and Gustave found a dry spot and curled themselves up, thinking of the consequences of the planned action. Soon their eyes closed and they were sleeping.

Gustave's Dream

"The railroad needs to get through that mountain," said the engineer. "Do you think you can blast a tunnel through that rock?"

Gustave replied, "I can blast anything with this improved blast stick formula that my partner Gill has developed. All you need to do is bore holes into the rock, so we can slide the long sticks down. Then we light the fuse and the rock will come tumbling down. All you need to do is shovel the pieces up and keep going into the side of that hill until we come out the other side."

"What about going from the other side and meet in the middle?" asked the engineer.

"Sure, we can do it both ways, but you'll need two crews to do it that way," replied Gustave.

The Legend of the Pikesville Cave

"We need to have this completed by year end and we don't have much time left. The Pennsylvania Railroad is anxious to complete this line. We need to do it fast and we have the manpower. Let's get started now," counseled the engineer.

"Wake up Gustave!"

Gill was shaking his friend. "They are bringing in an engine to couple up with the ammunition cars."

Gustave looked through his blurry eyes and saw the smoke puffing out the stack of the engine which was backing down from the left. The lieutenant was already loading

his musket. "We'll have to try detonating the blast sticks without the benefit of the daylight. Its just about dawn now and we can't wait."

They looked at the lieutenant, "What if we miss?"

"Then we just run for the woods. There won't be any blast to cover our escape. I think we should leave our muskets behind so as not to be encumbered as we take flight."

The engine was coming closer to the cars and a trainman had jumped to the ground to connect the couplers.

"Now, shoot!" said the lieutenant.

Gustave took aim, and on the count of three, all three muskets fired at once. The Minié balls hurtled to their marks as if in slow motion. Would they hit the blast sticks before the engine jarred the cars and spoiled their targets? Would they have to drop their muskets and run for their lives? Would the enemy see them? Would they be killed?

All three Minié balls hit simultaneously with deadly accuracy. The blast sticks erupted with a roar, sending shrapnel in all directions. The ammunition in the railroad cars began to fire off, adding to the conflagration. The scene was general mayhem.

"Let's vamoose, corporals," advised the lieutenant. They stared in wide-eyed amazement and disbelief at the havoc they wreaked. Then they ran into the woods while parts of the ammunition train were still raining down all around them. They were lucky not to be hit by the debris. They ran faster and faster and soon were out of range of the explosion.

They heard the bugler sound the alarm at the Confederate camp and they knew that they would be pursued in a few minutes or as soon as the area was clear enough for the enemy to get through the rubble and the exploding ordinance. They had a good head start, ran fast, and had reached the place where the haversacks were stored in less than ten minutes.

As agreed, the other six men of their platoon had already doubled up and carried the corporals' and the lieutenant's haversacks to give them an advantage in their flight from the fight.

"We still have a day's march ahead of us. We might catch up with the others in the platoon, but that's not important.

The Legend of the Pikesville Cave

I think we have put a big thorn in the side of General Van Dorn's army," said the lieutenant. We drove them out of Missouri and soon we'll keep them out for good."

~~~~~~~

But Major General Earl Van Dorn had other ideas. He had reorganized the Confederate army that had been driven south, and, despite the loss of his reserve artillery ammunition in an explosion, he planned a counter-offensive. He hoped his victory would enable the Confederates to recapture northern Arkansas and Missouri. He had a superior army by the numbers, with nearly twice as many men as the Union.

~~~~~~~

Sergeant Cliff, along with Corporals Rupert, Jerry, Stephen, Alexander, and Joseph, trudged along the nearly frozen road back toward camp. At about noon, they sighted the columns of General Sigel's First and Second Divisions heading in their direction followed by the Third and Fourth Divisions commanded by General Curtis.

The six men of the SD Platoon picked up their pace, and when they were within shouting distance of the columns, began to run. Captain Morgan, on his horse and recognizing his men, left the formation and galloped toward them.

"At ease, men," he shouted over the clamor of the marching troops. "What have you to report?"

The sergeant spoke, "There are nearly 20,000 Confederates by our reckoning, **sir**. We blew up their artillery ammunition train with the new blast sticks. The six of us planted the sticks and the lieutenant and Gustave and Gill set them off. We heard the explosion. They are back a ways catching up. There is an excellent defensive position along a stream. We suggest you take the troops there."

80   Chapter 6 The Battle of Pea Ridge

"Good work men," acknowledged the captain. "Now wait here while I report your news. Then fall in behind me back in the formation. I'll get this to General Sigel immediately."

The captain wheeled his horse around and headed to the command party at the head of the columns, where the general and his staff rode. After a few minutes, he rejoined the march in his position. As he passed, the six men of SD Platoon fell in behind him as they were instructed.

By sunset, all four divisions were entrenched on the north side of Little Sugar Creek, ready for the battle they expected the next day. The SD Platoon was positioned near the command tent and was not active in the battle, except to observe and record. They had done their job and deserved this inactivity. The battle itself is best reported from local newspaper description that was published in **The Bentonville Gazette** on March 9, 1862.

~~~~~~~

While they fought well together on the battlefield, General Curtis and General Sigel did not get along well. Sigel was somewhat of an arrogant, stubborn "kraut" and claimed the Pea Ridge victory as if it belonged to him and his German troops. That was not very politic, and Curtis, while equal in rank, managed to have Sigel transferred East with less responsibility as commander of troops in the Shenandoah Valley of Pennsylvania. Still, Sigel was promoted to the rank of Major General near the end of March. However, he did not participate in any major battles after Pea Ridge. Sigel took many of his most trusted and skilled platoons, including SD Platoon, with him to Pennsylvania.

The Bentonville Gazette

VOL. 20 NO. 9 — **MARCH 9, 1862**

Confederates Driven From Missouri
by Stanley Billistein

Generals Curtis and Sigel commanding over 10,000 Union troops from Iowa, Indiana, Illinois, Missouri, and Ohio marched their way into Arkansas on March 6 and set up a defensive position along the north side of Little Sugar Creek where they successfully drove off the larger Confederate force commanded by General Van Dorn.

Key to this victory was the absence of Van Dorn's artillery ammunition that was destroyed early in the morning of March 5. While sabotage is suspected, it remains a mystery how the three supply rail cars could have been so utterly obliterated by mere blasting powder.

With the opposing guns rendered nearly harmless, Sigel directed his gunners to fire into the woods at the Confederate infantry near the base of Big Mountain. The projectiles created a deadly combination of rock shrapnel and wood splinters, driving the 2nd Missouri Brigade from its positions. The Southern commander bitterly realized that he had no hope of victory and decided to retreat via the Huntsville Road. A great cry of "Victory" was sent up around noon on March 8 near Elkhorn Tavern.

Part 4

War and Peace

Chapter 8
The Shenandoah Valley and the End of the War

By the time Major General Franz Sigel and his trusted platoons reached the Shenandoah Valley in eastern Pennsylvania, spring had begun to blossom into summer.

"The general does not seem pleased with his new assignment, for what that assignment is worth," grumbled the captain as he spoke with Lieutenant Chester.

"Yes, but he still is very successful at recruiting German Immigrants to the Union's cause. President Lincoln must be a fan of that aspect of old Sigel. Remember, the president himself had promoted him to the rank of brigadier general a while back even before our latest battle," replied Chester. "And then after his stellar performance *at* Pea Ridge, he was moved up to major general. Don't forget that," added the lieutenant.

"But his men are getting restless. In a way, they miss the action," continued the captain.

In another tent, in the enlisted section of Sigel's camp, sat Gustave and Gill. It had been some time since they had seen any action besides marching. True, they practiced their sharpshooting every day, but it was the blast sticks

85

86 Chapter 7 The Shenandoah Valley and the End of the War

they missed the most. "We need to blow something up," said Gill with a gleam in his eye.

~~~~~~~

A few days later, Lieutenant Chester gathered his men. Something was afoot. "Men, we have a different kind of job to do. It's not soldiering in the sense of killing the enemy, or taking prisoners, or blowing up supply trains. We will be on loan for some time to the Army Corps of Engineers."

"Why us, Sir?" piped up Gill.

"Corporal, it's because of you and your blast sticks. Or should I call them those *blasted* sticks," replied Lieutenant Chester. "There is the side of a mountain that is in the way of a railroad line they are building. They need it blasted away. They have tried blasting powder but the mountain is just too tough."

"Will ordinance and quartermaster be coming too?" asked Gustave. "We need them to make the blast sticks."

"The Corps has their own ordinance and they can certainly get the supplies. We'll have to teach them how to make the blast sticks. We'll set the explosives off," responded the lieutenant. "I'm sure they will learn fast and then they will probably take over the entire operation and leave us out in the cold, so to speak. But we have been assigned this task and we board a train tomorrow morning. So pack up and be ready at 7 o'clock."

The eight member of Platoon SD were ready the night before and slept restlessly in their tents. When the sun was just breaking above the horizon, they trudged down to breakfast with their haversacks, muskets and backpacks loaded with the few sticks of explosive they had saved from their previous expedition at Pea Ridge. Gustave had the detonators and fuses that had not been needed or used still in his backpack.

The train headed north toward the Appalachian Mountains where the work needed to be done. It was nearly three in the afternoon when the engine came to a stop. It was the end of the line. There was no more track. And, directly ahead, they could see a large rocky obstruction in their path.

"This must be it," exclaimed Lieutenant Chester as an Army Corps of Engineers officer stuck his head into the car that housed SD Platoon. "Welcome to the end of the line," he said. "Take a load off your feet after you set up your tents. Follow me. It's not too far a walk."

They followed the Corps lieutenant to a clearing where there were a dozen tents set up. Just beyond those tents were larger structures and machinery the likes of which they had never seen before. Some machines were steaming and making chugging sounds.

"Here we are," advised the lieutenant. "For now, just drop your stuff. I want to show you our problem close up. I hope your fabled blast sticks can solve it."

They carefully dropped their packs and haversacks in a clear spot, and stacked their muskets. Then they followed the lieutenant toward the machinery. Some of the machines were on narrow gauge railroad track and they could see that the track was set up so that after work had been accomplished, they could move on to the next part of the project. However based on the entrenched look of the machinery, it appeared that it had not been moved for some time.

88 Chapter 7 The Shenandoah Valley and the End of the War

The lieutenant began as he pointed to the outcropping of rock, "You have probably observed that we are stuck right here. This rock is extremely solid and our steam drills have not been able to do more than just bore holes into it. Blasting powder only makes a dent in this rock. We have thought of using nitro, but it is far too dangerous to handle."

Lieutenant Chester spoke up, "That's why we devised the blast sticks. They contain nitro, but the nitro is absorbed by the sawdust and is safe to handle. We did some experiments to determine the safety as well as the effectiveness of our blast sticks."

"Yes, we heard of your work at Pea Ridge and that's why we called you in to help," responded the lieutenant. "By the way, I forgot to introduce myself in my excitement. I'm Lieutenant Frank Goss. Welcome to the *Short Line RR,* as we have nicknamed it. It's supposed to extend up to New York's Erie Canal and serve as a major Union supply line for the war effort farther south. It was supposed to be completed a month ago, but we ran into this confounded hard rock."

It was getting late and Lieutenant Goss led them back to the main camp. They pitched their tents and got settled in. The summer sun was still above the horizon and supper was still cooking.

Lieutenant Chester spoke up, "I think we have enough time to try a blast stick in one of the holes you have drilled into the rock. Gustave get a detonator out and a long fuse. Rupert, do you have a blast stick or two ready? Let's give it a try before supper."

They returned to the spot where the steam drill had made a number of holes in the rock. "How far down do these holes go?" asked Chester.

The Legend of the Pikesville Cave

"About five feet. Then the drill quits," replied Goss.

"The hole looks like it's about the diameter of three blast sticks," reasoned Chester. "Bundle three sticks together and to make sure they all detonate. Gustave, put detonators and fuses in all of them."

The men did their jobs and soon the package was ready to slide down the hole. They pushed it with a stick much like the way they pushed the Minié ball down the barrel of their musket. However, they were careful not to break the fuse.

"Ready, Sir," reported Gustave.

"Light her up," commanded Lieutenant Chester.

Gustave opened his tinder box and struck a match, held it to the fuse, watched it take, and as it fizzed, he ran like the devil was chasing him. They all watched from the shelter of a makeshift barrier that the Army Corps had erected when they used blasting powder. Of course, the powder had no effect. The fuse burned up to the hole and then the glow disappeared into the hole. "Five feet to go," said Gustave. "It should blow in 10, 9, 8, 7, 6, 5, 4, 3, 2, 1 now," he counted backwards.

There was a tremendous boom and a huge sheet of stone went flying off the side of the mountain, along with many smaller rocks, and a giant dust cloud formed. The shelter was inundated with smaller stones and a huge amount of dust. No one was injured, but they were covered in gray. One piece of rock hit a machine and crushed it into the ground. "That was too close, and we look like Confederates in all this gray dust!" exclaimed Lieutenant Goss. "We'll have to move the machinery back out of the range of the debris. But look, it worked! We cleared more mountain in this one evening than we did all last month. We have a solution! Gentlemen, thank you."

90 Chapter 7 The Shenandoah Valley and the End of the War

Supper that evening was a jubilant affair. There were many handshakes and pats on the back of the eight members of SD Platoon by the Army Corps who had been on this difficult job for weeks. They now knew they had a solution to the problem and to problems that would inevitably crop up in the future with impenetrable rock. Gill's blast sticks had once again proven themselves.

Gill and Gustave retired to their tent and, due to the excitement of the day, found it hard to sleep.

"Gill," said Gustave. "You asleep?"

Gill replied, "No. I can't sleep. I keep thinking about that blast today."

"You know, I never did hear about your life in Germany except that your father was killed in a nitro explosion. Remember, you were about to tell me after I told you my story," reminded Gustave.

Gill began as he had before, "My mother (Hildegarde) is German and my father (Emil) was Swedish. Just the opposite of your parents. My father, you recall, was the younger brother of my Uncle Alfred Nobel. Uncle Al was an interesting man. His father and mother made sure he was educated, but they lost a fortune shortly after Uncle Al graduated from university. But that did not stop him. With his book learning, he was able to begin again. His specialty was chemistry and mechanical engineering. My father worked for him and one of my father's first jobs was to sell Uncle Al's products in Germany, which as you know is just across a short bit of the Baltic Sea. In fact, that's from where we departed on our way over here to America.

"On one of his business trips, he met my mother in a tavern where she was working as a serving girl. He must have been attracted to her, because he returned on the next trip

The Legend of the Pikesville Cave

to that same tavern. In fact, he returned many times over the course of a year. By then, my mother was pregnant with me and while my Uncle Al disapproved of the marriage, my father insisted. The wedding was in July and I was born on December 25, 1843. I don't know why they did not call me some other more Christmassy name like Christopher, but Gilbert is my name. I got my nickname because I could swim like a fish.

"I was eleven when my father met with his terrible accident. At first, Uncle Al seemed to be sympathetic and he offered to look after me and my mother in Sweden. That's where I got to see him in his plant as he worked on the blasting sticks with his employees. He made his money by selling munitions to governments and designing civil engineering works like bridges. While he was well off, I don't know if we were a burden on his resources, or if he still did not like my mother. I was fifteen when he had us shipped back to my mother's village in Germany. We had some money, but it soon ran out, and that's why I signed up for a mercenary job in this American war."

Gustave shuffled in his sleeping bag, "That's quite a story. Seems both of our fates are tied up in war or some aspect of it."

"Yes, it seems that humans are always in some kind of conflict. I had the chance to get some schooling while I lived with Uncle Al. In history class we learned about the really ancient wars between the Greeks and the Trojans. They did not have the modern weapons we have today and had to fight with swords and their bare hands," Gill yawned. "Good night Gustave."

Gustave was slowly falling asleep. It had been a big day.

Morning came fast. The summer sun had just risen and the camp was bustling with activity. The civilian workmen

92 Chapter 7 The Shenandoah Valley and the End of the War

had already had breakfast and were heading to the steam drill. Gustave, Gill, and the other members of their platoon were shown the coffee pot and there was a healthy breakfast of freshly harvested fruit ready for them.

Lieutenant Goss came over to where they were finishing up their meal.

"How many blast sticks do you still have?" he asked.

Lieutenant Chester replied, "We had about a dozen left from our Pea Ridge escapade. We used three yesterday, so I would say we have about nine left."

"Can you make any more? I think we need a lot more than nine to complete this job," said Goss.

"That all depends on what supplies you have here. Do you have any nitro? We also need fine sawdust, and sodium carbonate, and tubes to hold the mixture. I'm sure you have fuses and we can fabricate the detonators with blasting powder which I'm sure you have lots of."

Lieutenant Goss thought for a minute and then told them there was a small supply of nitro in the ordinance tent. He was not aware of any sodium carbonate, but they had, as Chester had thought, a lot of blasting powder. Tubes they could make with paper wrapped multiple times around itself.

Gill interjected, "Sir, we could make the sodium carbonate from baking soda like we did when we first made the blast sticks."

"Right," echoed Lieutenant Chester.

Lieutenant Goss thought a minute and then said, "I'll send the supply train back to HQ, where there is a good supply of nitro. We have a special car with shock absorbing rigging to hold the explosive and we run the train very slowly with a long draw bar between it and the engine. It does an excellent job of moving the nitro with no explosions - so far."

The Legend of the Pikesville Cave

"Great," observed Chester. "Meanwhile, we can blast away at least three more times with the sticks we have with us. That should extend your *Short Line RR* a few hundred feet."

The part of the civilian crew that had set off to the work area, was busy clearing the rock from the blast of the night before. Another group was starting up the drill which had just come up to steam. It was wedged into an area and anchored to the ground. The crew started drilling. It was possible to see the auger bite into the rock and begin a hole. The idea was to get a hole in the side of the hill big enough to hold a charge and then blow the stubborn rock out and create a vertical cliff side. The rock was so hard and the drilling would take a few hours.

SD Platoon sat down and began to plan their strategy. They would need a supply of fine sawdust. Rupert and Jerry found a two man saw and some hard wood and began making the fine sawdust, which was collected under the sawing on a tarp. Stephen went off to the kitchen to see if the cook had any baking soda. They would need a few pounds to make the sodium carbonate in an oven at 200 degrees F. It might mean no biscuits for a few days until more baking soda arrived on the train with the nitro. That train moved so very slowly! The train would also be bringing the heavy paper to make the cylinders and a quantity of wax to seal the ends. It looked like they were in the blast stick manufacturing business. "The Short Line RR will soon become the Long Line RR," they joked as they went about their business.

Gill and Gustave, with the rest of the SD platoon personnel, began to work on the construction of a suitable building to make the blast sticks. They set the foundation as far

94 Chapter 7 The Shenandoah Valley and the End of the War

back from the demolition zone as possible so that any rock debris from the blasts would not fall on the sensitive materials that would be stored there. They figured that once the blast sticks were made, they could be safely moved to the next blasting site by foot or, when the sites were farther away, on the train. Camp would stay in the current location for at least a few weeks.

The first part of the day went smoothly and dinner was a welcome break from the tiring work of that morning. The train had departed early to get the supplies, but was not expected until the weekend which was four days away.

Right after dinner, the steam drill crew told Lieutenant Goss that the hole was about five feet deep. It was time to use the next three sticks to blow the rock off the face of the hill. Gustave and the rest of the platoon went to the hole, where Gustave set up the detonators and the fuse. This time, the blast was not quite so powerful, or the rock may have been harder, but no giant slab was blown off. There was just an indentation in the side of the hill. The steam drill was located down a few yards from the newly blasted spot and the process began again.

"Too bad we don't have more than one steam drill," complained Gill. "We could drill multiple holes and fire off more blast sticks at the same time. That may create a super additive effect."

"I agree," observed Lieutenant Goss. "I'll get on that and telegraph our need for two more drills and have them on the train when it returns. You fellows are certainly wise. It's good to have you around."

The rest of the day dragged on as they waited for the steam drill to complete the hole. Again, they were able to make an indentation in the side of the hill and the civilian crew spent the remainder of the day cleaning up the debris with shovels and pickaxes. By evening, just before supper, there was enough flat ground to begin laying down new ties and rails. They had made a dent in the rock obstacle and the railroad was on its way. They slept well that night.

~~~~~~~

Progress continued, but the blast sticks that SD Platoon had brought with them ran out at the end of the third day. The weekend when the train was scheduled to arrive was still a day away.

It was getting hot during the day, and there was nothing much to do except maybe watch the steam drill crew labor away. It was like watching grass grow.

One of the reasons the roadbed for the railroad track had to be fitted along the side of the hard rock mountain was the direction of the route along a valley that had been formed by a river. This was the narrowest part of the valley, actually a small canyon at this point. Most of the riverbed ran through soft soil and the erosion the river created a wide expanse of relatively flat ground.

But this particular part of the countryside was much harder than what had been fertile farmland.

Gill asked Lieutenant Goss, who had studied geology at West Point, "What made this hill so hard?"

96 Chapter 7 The Shenandoah Valley and the End of the War

"We are not sure, but this could have been an ancient volcano. The only thing that puts a damper on this theory is that volcanic rock is never this hard," replied Lieutenant Goss. "Whatever the reason for this hard rock, there is a cool river down there and I'm hot and dusty. Let's go for a swim.

"Everybody, stop work. You all deserve a swim on this hot day. We have made good progress this week. The nitro has not arrived yet. So take the rest of the afternoon off. You've earned it."

The workmen quickly tore off their dirty clothes and the soldiers removed their uniforms and stripped to nothing. The water was cool, but not cold, and soon they were all up to their necks as they waded out into the deep flowing stream. It felt good to get clean and the sun was still high, so they went back to the shore and brought their clothes back for a good washing. There were no trees nearby to hang the wet laundry on, so they had to carry them to camp, where they rigged makeshift clothes lines off tent poles.

~~~~~~~

The newly washed clothes were a bit stiff the next morning. Those who did not have extra clothes had slept naked. The night air was warm and they didn't even need any blanket cover. When they put their clean shirts and pants on over their underwear, they had to crumple them over and over a few times to get the stiffness out. But it was good to have clean, fresh clothes. Summer was a special time of the year. The aroma of a fresh breakfast filled their noses and they all, civilians and soldiers alike, trooped off to the mess tent. As they finished the last of the bacon and eggs, they could hear the puff-chug of the engine as it labored up the incline toward the camp.

"Hear the train? Nitro will be here soon," observed Lieutenant Goss. "We will meet it down the track on the siding where the engine will uncouple from the last car. That car has the nitro. The rest of the train will head up to the station near the camp and the remaining supplies will be unloaded there. This is the safest way to deliver such dangerous material to a location that is a good distance from camp. Now let's get going!"

The eight members of the platoon plus Lieutenants Goss and Chester hiked the half mile to the siding and arrived just in time to see the engine pulling in. It was chugging along very slowly as it negotiated the turn from the main line and headed into the siding. As it turned back through the second track switch with a passenger coach and three freight cars followed by three flatcars, it slowed to a crawl and then stopped. "The final box car has the nitro in it and the brakeman will uncouple it when it has cleared the first turnout," said Lieutenant Goss. "Then the rest of the train will continue to camp."

The brakeman did his job and the front part of the train pulled ahead and into camp. While the train was stopped for uncoupling, a small group of soldiers got off the passenger car and joined the group. It was the ordinance crew who had worked with SD Platoon back in Si-

98 Chapter 7 The Shenandoah Valley and the End of the War

gel's camp. Lieutenant Swartz, the chemist, led this small group. Now there were three lieutenants and their men working on the effort to blast the hard rock, and prepare the rail line to get supplies from the factories in New York to the battlefields.

Lieutenant Swartz spoke first. "So you need some help making blast sticks. Well, we have done that a number of times and with great success. It was our blasters that destroyed the Rebels artillery ammunition train before the Pea Ridge battle. O yes, and SD Platoon had a little bit to do with that too. I see they are here."

Lieutenant Chester mumbled something under his breath but did not challenge the haughty statement of Swartz.

He said out loud, "Let's get on with the blast stick fabrication. The steam drill has probably bored ten holes in the rock by now."

Swartz chimed in, "We should build our blast stick fabrication hut right here close to the nitro. That way we won't have to transport it very far."

"But we can store the finished blast sticks on the other side of camp closer to the blasting zone where we need them," advised Goss. "I'm in charge of the total effort to get this damned mountain demolished."

~~~~~~~

The work progressed well. A hut was hastily constructed and ordinance began to fill the wax coated paper sticks with a mixture of sawdust and sodium carbonate. Then the nitro would be added very carefully.

A balance was used to weigh out the sawdust/carbonate mixture that was sufficient to fill the empty stick. Then

The Legend of the Pikesville Cave

99

three times the weight of this sawdust mixture would be weighed out of the nitro flask, into a glass beaker and the height of the nitro marked on the side of the breaker.

The nitro would be then added from this beaker to the stick that had the sawdust in it. This was the delicate job. If the nitro was added too quickly, there was a real danger of an explosion. In the summer heat, the nitro was far less viscous than it was in the cold of winter when the crew made the last batch of blast sticks. This "runny nitro" presented a new challenge for Billy, the soldier who was pouring the dangerous liquid.

"This stuff is a lot more liq..... **BLAST!** .....went the nitro as Billy poured too quickly.

The hut was flattened and Billy with it. Gill ran toward the devastation and tried to pull Billy out of the rubble, but there was nothing to take hold of. Billy was completely gone.

"Are you all right, Gill?" asked Lieutenant Chester.

"A slight burn on my left hand," replied Gill

"Get yourself to the medic," urged Chester.

~~~~~~~

There was no laughter that day nor night and none for the next whole week. A weak attempt was made to reconstruct the blast stick fabrication hut, but the men had no spirit. They had lost a good friend. The members of the ordinance platoon were especially devastated, and at Billy's funeral they sang a new song that had just been published.

100 Chapter 7 The Shenandoah Valley and the End of the War

**Mine eyes have seen the glory of the coming of the Lord;
He is trampling out the vintage where the grapes of wrath are stored;
He hath loosed the fateful lightning of His terrible swift sword:
His truth is marching on.**

**Glory, glory, hallelujah!
Glory, glory, hallelujah!
Glory, glory, hallelujah!
His truth is marching on.**

*Here lies Billy Burke
Who Died Making Blast Sticks
May He Rest In Peace*

*Your Friends
Chester
Cliff
Gustave
Gill
Rupert
Jerry
Stephen
Alexander
Joseph*

They slowly marched in rank and file to the grave where the remains of Billy were buried by the undertaker. A small gravestone was placed on the grave which was signed by all the members of the platoon.

The Legend of the Pikesville Cave 101

Back in their tent about a week later, Gustave and Gill sadly reflected on the events that led up to the explosion. "It could have been any of us," said Gill with a tremble in his voice.

Gustave thought for a bit and then added, "It was so easy to make the blast sticks in February and March. What do you suppose happened last week?"

"I hope Lieutenant Swartz can come up with a solution to this problem," continued Gill. "We need the sticks to finish this blasted railroad. The Rebels are advancing north and our Union armies need the supplies to hold them off and to drive them back."

They both drifted off in a restless sleep.

Gustave's Dream

The railroad had run into a stone wall in an area just a few miles south of York, Pennsylvania. It was typical of the work Gustave had done over and over in the five years since his discharge from the army. Get a steam drill to bore holes in the rock. Slide the dynamite sticks down the holes and set them off. Dynamite was the new explosive that was a vast improvement over the crude blast sticks he had used in the war. It was being manufactured by a big arms company in Delaware, The E. I. duPont de Nemours and Company.

As the side of the mountain slowly gave way to the Dynamite Gustave began to see holes in the rock. Soon these holes revealed a huge cavern with strange bluish rock formations hung from the ceiling that was at least a hundred feet high. The formations were dripping water and there were formations on the floor of the cave directly below the upper drippers.

102 Chapter 7 The Shenandoah Valley and the End of the War

It looked like the cave went right through the mountain. This would be an easy tunnel since Mother Nature had done most of the work already, he thought. His only worry was if there was a cave-in.

He directed his crew to the other side of the mountain and they began to blast there. After a few days, they were back inside the cave from the other direction and the tunnel was completed.

~~~~~~~

"Gill, I just had the most exciting dream," exclaimed Gustave as he opened his eyes and saw the first faint beams of sunlight creep across the camp which was just beginning to stir. "I dreamt that I had blasted a tunnel in a mountain with improved blast sticks called **dynamite**. The tunnel was really a cave with strange formations on the ceiling and on the floor."

"Uncle Al had used that word **dynamite** once or twice when I was with him. I wonder how you dreamed it up?" replied Gill. "But that cave sounds interesting. Do you think we'll ever find such a phenomenon? I remember a name for that type of exploring from back home. I think it's called *Spelunking*. But let's get going, we still need to make some blast sticks and we don't want to blast ourselves doing so. I wonder if Lieutenant Swartz will have any ideas when he gets back from HQ on the train today?"

Breakfast was a bit more lively than the previous week as the men began to adjust to the realities of war and the inevitability of death. However unnecessary, avoidable death like Billy's was not the norm and this would be a burden they would carry for many weeks. The steam drill crew

The Legend of the Pikesville Cave

had already resumed work and there were many holes in the mountainside waiting for the blast sticks. IF THEY COULD BE MADE!

Lieutenants Goss, Chester, and Swartz had gone off to HQ and arrived that morning just after breakfast with some information and possible new techniques to make blast sticks.

Swartz began the meeting with the SD Platoon and the Corps of Engineers, "Nitro freezes at about 50 degrees F, so it was very thick in the cold of February when we made the first batch of blast sticks. In July heat, nitro is a very watery liquid and is not very stable when poured. We were lucky to get it out of the big container in the boxcar when we did in the early morning before the sun was up, otherwise the whole boxcar would have blown up and all of us with it."

Lieutenant Chester continued relating the rest of the new information, "We need ice to cool the nitro and a method to drizzle it into the sawdust in the blast stick. We believe that if handled in a more viscous state and if it is poured more slowly, we can produce a good quantity of explosives. Enough to finish this job at least."

"Getting the ice is a problem," continued Swartz. If we had the track heading north it could come in on a special insulated railroad car. But the mountain is in the way!"

Sergeant Cliff interrupted, "We seem to be stuck between a rock and a hard place. To blast the mountain, we need to have blasted the mountain!"

Gustave suggested, "Why not blast from the other side of the mountain? Isn't the track already there?"

Gill interjected another idea, "Or why not float the ice down the river and haul it up here?"

104 Chapter 7 The Shenandoah Valley and the End of the War

"I think Gill has something!" exclaimed Jerry and Rupert simultaneously. "Ice comes in big blocks. We come from New England where Fred Tudor's company mines ice in the winter and ships it all over the world."

"Can ordinance get some ice down here, Swartz?" asked Goss.

"That's a job for the quartermaster," replied Swartz. "I'll contact the quartermaster in the main camp on the telegraph right now and get his butt

Ice harvesting at Spy Pond - Public Domain

in gear. We'll get that ice delivered on the other side of the mountain and we'll float it down stream!"

Swartz was quite effective and had the promise of ice in a fortnight. He explained, "That's the best I could do. It will take a few days to find the ice in Massachusetts and move it to New York by train. Then a few more days to send it through New York on the Erie Canal and then at least one day on a special train down here. We can meet the train on the other side by wading upstream. Since ice floats, we can guide it down the river in less than half a day. If we get it in ten days, we'll be doing well."

"Won't the ice melt in the river?" asked Joseph.

"The river is not warm, as you know from the swim we all took the other day. We should have enough ice to do the job if we are ready when it arrives. I have ordered a ton of ice," replied Swartz.

The camp was alive with the anticipation of the arrival of the ice. A new fabrication hut was built. This time it was

The Legend of the Pikesville Cave

constructed with a steel framework with chunks of rock that were held together with strong mortar. This construction took a few days which helped pass the time while the ice was on its way.

A clever opening was built into the side of the hut and a special burette was set up with a stand on a table in the hut. Through that clever opening, a rod was attached to the burette's stopcock and the stopcock could be turned remotely by the operator on the outside of the hut and away from imminent danger. The army was fortunate to have a glass blower in a nearby town who could fabricate the specialized vessels they needed.

The SD Platoon spent the remainder of the waiting time making the blast sticks waxed paper housings. They had prepared over 100 tubes complete with the sawdust and sodium carbonate mixture. Now all they needed was the ice to cool the nitro. Each stick would be placed in a holder directly under the burette that was filled with chilled nitro from a container mounted above it. Then the nitro would be slowly drizzled into the tube and the nitro would mix into the sawdust/carbonate mixture. The blast stick would be removed from the holder and a new empty tube inserted into the holder. The procedure would be repeated until all the nitro had been made safe in the blast sticks.

It was Gill's job to fill the burette and then drizzle the nitro into the stick. The whole operation would take about five minutes per stick and the rest of the crew were involved with placing an empty stick in the holder and removing the finished blast sticks. Gustave was Gill's backup and watched over his friend like a hawk. Lieutenant Chester was like a mother hen to his men. He did

106 Chapter 7 The Shenandoah Valley and the End of the War

not want any more funerals, especially a funeral for his men. They practiced the operation until it was down pat.

Soon the waiting game was over and the ice was only a half mile away. That was the half mile of mountain they needed to blast away with the sticks they were making. They needed the ice to cool the nitro so it would not blow up as they made the sticks. It was a convoluted process with many *if's*, many of which could result in disaster.

If the ice did not cool the nitro sufficiently, it would explode when it was poured into the stick. If the pouring was too rapid, the nitro would explode. If the ice cooled the nitro too much, it would freeze and not be liquid enough to drizzle into the stick. But now it was time to get the ice. That was the first part of a carefully laid plan.

Everybody wanted to get into the river and float the big blocks of ice to camp. They worked their way upstream against the current which was strong, but not impossible to buck. It took about an hour to navigate and as soon as they were in sight of the shore, the train crew began to unload the freight car. The ice had been packed in sawdust to keep it from melting and was very dirty before it came in contact with the water. It took a team of three men to wrangle the large blocks of ice that must have weighed 250 pounds each. They had picks and ropes to help the process. The current made the ride easier than the upstream battle they had experienced getting to the freight car. Only one block got away and floated rapidly downstream past the camp and out of useful range. However, they had a lot of ice even though in the fifteen minute flotilla nearly half had melted in the water. Using block and tackle and a lot of just plain muscle, the blocks of ice were pulled up on the shore and then safely housed in the ice house they had

The Legend of the Pikesville Cave

built. This house had thick walls and was insulated with piles of coarse sawdust that the crew had been making as they waited for the shipment to arrive.

"Take a rest, men," commanded Lieutenant Chester. "We'll set up the cooling tub right after dinner when you are rested and able to do the job with finesse and steady hands."

When dinner was over and the men felt refreshed and warmed up after their mile of cold water ice handling, they said they were ready to tackle the biggest and most dangerous part of the project - moving the nitroglycerine and the final set up of the fabrication hut. If they succeeded and did not blow themselves to kingdom come, they would have, by day's end, enough blasting sticks to finish "shaving" the mountain and making the right-of-way clear for the track and the supply trains. The first thing they did was to prepare a cooling tub that would hold the large flask of nitroglycerine that was still in the box car on the nearby siding. In the July heat, it is a wonder that it had not already spontaneously exploded. They brought the tub into the car and gingerly placed it below the flask.

The flask with the large quantity of nitroglycerine was carefully lowered from its suspension in the freight car into the tub of ice that had been chopped into two inch pieces from one of the big blocks. They watched as the nitro begin to freeze at the edges of the flask. Soon it was nearly frozen all the way to the center of the flask. They removed the slings that had supported the flask of nitro on its trip from the main camp.

There were two poles going through the tub's handles. Joseph and Alexander took hold of the ends of the poles inside the freight car and Rupert and Jerry held the ends of the poles over their heads outside the car. As they lifted the heavy object, they slowly moved the tub and nitro so it was now outside the car. Stephen and Cliff relieved Joseph and Alexander of their ends as the poles emerged from the door of the box car. Slowly the procession, much like that of pallbearers at a funeral, moved the high explosive toward the fabrication hut. It was difficult to hold the tub and flask of nitro above their heads, and the change of guard came in as planned to lower it to a hip level grip which was less of a strain. Joseph and Alexander took the front and Gustave and Gill took the back.

The fabrication hut had a slanted incline and the "funeral procession" began to ascend to the open roof area. The poles had been measured to fit exactly into groves in the top of the open roof area. "On the count of three," commanded Lieutenant Chester. "One, two, three," he shouted out and the four pallbearers slowly lowered the tub into its position and the poles were fit into the slots. Everything fit perfectly and the spigot at the bottom of the tub (which had a hole cut into it) was exactly above the burette that would be used to measure the precise amount of nitro for each blast stick.

The Legend of the Pikesville Cave 109

The nitro began to warm up enough to begin the procedure. The first empty blast stick had already been placed in the holder below the burette when the apparatus had been set up initially. Gill gingerly attached the remote control pole to the spigot on the bottom of the flask of nitro and turned the handle. The cold nitro began to slowly drizzle into the burette and when it reached the mark that signaled the correct amount, he shut the spigot off. A few more lingering drops went into the burette. "I'll have to shut it off just a tad sooner to prevent too much nitro from going into the measuring burette," observed Gill. "But those few drops are not enough to make a difference."

Now the nitro was warming fast and Gill had to release it into the blast stick. This is where Billy had done it too fast and met his fate.

Gill turned the spigot on the burette and the nitro began to drizzle as they had planned into the sawdust filled stick. In about a minute it was filled and Joseph advanced to the fabrication hut, removed the loaded blast stick from the holder, and placed a blank stick in its place. Joseph walked to the storage hut far away from the fabrication hut and deposited the newly made blast stick. Alexander was next to remove the live blast stick and deposit another blank. As Gill filled the burette and drizzled the nitro into

110 Chapter 7 The Shenandoah Valley and the End of the War

the blanks, making them live, the entire crew rotated the process of removing the live one and replacing it with a blank. Gill was getting a bit weary toward the end of the day, but all of the nitro had been used and the storage hut was full of newly made blast sticks. They had done the job without a mishap. Tomorrow, they would begin blasting the mountain.

~~~~~~

Gustave and Gill and the rest of SD Platoon returned to General Sigel's main camp by the end of July. They had made another major contribution to the Union's war effort. However, General Sigel had not been making a good name for himself. While his scout and demolition platoon had been blasting mountains in Northern Pennsylvania, Sigel had been defeated by Major General Thomas J. "Stonewall" Jackson, who managed to outwit Siegel's larger Union force.

In the Second Battle of Bull Run, General Sigel was wounded in the hand in this Union setback when General John Pope's army was defeated. Siegel's reputation as a general had eroded and he was considered inept. During the battle of Frederiksberg his troops were held in reserve. However, he still had a gift for recruiting German immigrants, which kept him in the favor of President Lincoln.

Lincoln had Sigel appointed to the new Department of West Virginia by Secretary of War Edwin M. Stanton. In his new command, Sigel opened the Valley

The Legend of the Pikesville Cave

Campaigns of 1864, launching an invasion of the Shenandoah Valley. He was soundly defeated by Maj. Gen. John C. Breckenridge at the Battle of New Market, on May 15, 1864, which was particularly embarrassing due to the prominent role young cadets from the Virginia Military Institute played in his defeat.

But all of this political intrigue was far from the two friends who met on a riverboat in Germany. They continued to do their scouting duties and often brought important information to Captain Morgan who still regarded this platoon as one of the finest he had ever commanded.

Probably the most important scouting information Captain Morgan received from SD Platoon was the alert that a large contingent of Confederate troops were marching along the old Chambersburg Pike toward a small village which was called Cashtown. The tiny village of Cashtown, Pennsylvania was nestled in the wooded slope of the Cashtown Gap in South Mountain. Gill and Gustave in civilian disguises had spoken with the Cashtown Innkeeper, Jacob Mickley who said, "..it appeared as if the entire force under Lee passed within twenty feet of my barroom."

Cashtown Inn Veranda

SD Platoon's report triggered the deployment of The Army of the Potomac, commanded by General Meade, who saw Lee attempting to penetrate the North again. While Cashtown was on one of the many supply roads, only eight miles away was Gettysburg at the center of the crossroads

Chapter 7 The Shenandoah Valley and the End of the War

and a strategic position for any army that wanted to invade the North. According to reports in the local newspapers after the battle, General Lee saw this advantage, and, convinced that his army was invincible, took an aggressive stand. Lee's beliefs were born out on the first and second day of battle and it looked as if the Confederacy would prevail in this important battle and go on to win the war.

But it was on the third day, July 3, 1863, that the Union artillery and infantry held fast and inflicted heavy losses on a charging Rebel force of 12,500 on Cemetery Ridge.

Lee's army of Northern Virginia was defeated and retreated in a seventeen mile long somber procession.

Gustave and Gill were fortunate. They were spared the heat of battle. Despite their sharpshooter rating, their assignment was to help with the wounded and, when the fighting was over, to bury the dead.

This had a profound effect on Gill more than any other experience of the war. He often was holding the hand of a mortally wounded soldier as the poor soul drifted off to an eternal reward. Gill learned to pray and to comfort his fellow soldiers from the Lutheran Chaplain, Rev. Morgan whom he befriended in those three gory days of battle and afterwards.

The South never invaded the North again and the war was over in less than two years.

The Legend of the Pikesville Cave 113

It is written that the South had little chance of winning the war despite the superior leadership of officers like General Lee. The North's powerful industrial machine and riches were just too much for the Confederacy which had only "King Cotton" to support its war machine. Because of blockades, cotton exports were cut to a trickle. The expected support for the Rebels by the European countries never materialized. The Confederate defeat at the Battle of Gettysburg made any hope of foreign support only wishful thinking. It would be a long twelve years of reconstruction before the nation was united again.

~~~~~~~

Gustave and Gill found themselves "out of work" so to speak. But they also were rich by the standards of the day. Their army pay amounted to $13 a month for a total of 44 months, or nearly $600.

"Gustave, what are you going to do with your pay?" asked Gill.

"I like this scouting and especially the demolition jobs where there are mountains to blast to make tunnels. I'm going into that line of work. I think I'll invest some of my pay in that DuPont Company. They are licensed to make your uncle's invention which is now called Dynamite. I might even start my own blasting company. How about you?"

"Since helping Rev. Morgan with the wounded and burying the dead, I have thought about doing something more spiritual with my life. I am going to study to become a minister. There is a Lutheran Seminary in Gettysburg. I have applied and I just got the letter of acceptance."

114 Chapter 7 The Shenandoah Valley and the End of the War

And so the two friends parted in early 1866. Gill had a short journey to Seminary Ridge where he began his studies.

His friend, Rev. Morgan, wished him the best and also said, "Gill, you are making a wise choice in your career. I have never regretted becoming a minister. You impressed me as a person capable of delivering much healing to your fellow man. I wish you the best in your studies."

Gustave's journey was quite a bit farther. He made an investment of $300 in DuPont stock and had it kept in a bank in Gettysburg. He used some of the money to buy a ticket on a train that was heading west. He heard that the army was looking for Indian scouts in Kansas and he headed to the western part of that state where the nomadic Indians hunted bison.

Part 5

Westward Ho!

Chapter 9
Scouting The West

Gustave's train pulled into Dodge City. It had been a long trip on the new AT&SF line that had been bringing settlers to the west for only a few months. Some of his fellow passengers were intending to buy land from the railroad and got a discount price on the ticket. If they did buy land, the price of their ticket would be deducted from the cost of the land. Gustave had paid the full price and had no intention of buying any land. He was here for employment at Fort Dodge as a scout. He had heard of other scouts doing this and he wanted to use his military training to good advantage. He also thought there may be an opportunity to use his blasting skills in extending the railroad lines.

When he arrived at Dodge City, "the city" was merely a sod hut. There weren't even any saloons, let alone a hotel to stay while he sought out employment by the army at the fort. He picked up his meager belongings which consisted of a change of clothing and the trusty musket that he'd purchased from the US Government for a mere $10 as "Army Surplus." He had an ample supply of ammunition and in his haversack, both sides of a pup tent. Gill had

118   Chapter 9 Scouting in the West

given him his side of the tent before he had enrolled in the seminary back in Gettysburg. That tent would come in handy that night as Gustave looked around for a suitable campsite. There were other campers on the Kansas plains that fateful night near the "metropolis" of Dodge City. He struck up a conversation with a fellow in buckskins who was a few years younger.

"Good evening sir." Gustave extended his hand.

"Howdy stranger. I'm Bill Cody. What's your handle?"

"I'm Gustave Pikestein. Fresh out of the Union Army and looking for work as an Indian Scout. I was a corporal and my training was in scouting and explosives."

"You came to the right place, my friend. I'm already scouting and I can put you in touch with the commander at Fort Dodge."

"That would be most kind of you sir," replied Gustave in his slightly German accent. He had overcome much of his struggle with the English language, but there was still a hint of his heritage in his voice. "Is there any water around here?"

"Over by the sod house there's a well, but the water is not fit for drinking unless you boil it first. OK to wash up in though. Gets the dust otta yer britches,.You got a pot fer boiling?"

"I do, and I have matches. I see tumbleweed. Does that make a good fire?"

"Sure does! We sometimes get prairie fires when a bunch of them weeds gets together and lightning strikes. Dig a

The Legend of the Pikesville Cave

shallow hole to keep the fire down flat and don't let it blow away. Cook on the glowing coals - not the big flames."

"Thanks again," Gustave said. "I got some coffee. Can I brew you up a cup?"

"It's a bit late in the day for me and coffee," said Bill. "But tomorrow morning, I'd love a fresh brewed cup. I'll bring my mug. See you then." Bill walked off.

Gustave pitched his tent which leaned down a bit since he only had one musket for a tent pole and there weren't any tree limbs in this nearly desert country. He boiled water from the well and made himself some coffee. He had become almost dependent on the brew.

He thought almost out loud, "Now for some supper."

He broke out some hardtack and pork. Soon the pork was sizzling in the frying pan, over the embers of the tumbleweed fire. He added the crumbled up hardtack. It was not the most appetizing supper, but with the coffee and sugar to wash it down he was not hungry.

As the sun went down in the west, he saw the stars begin to pop out of the moonless sky. He had never seen such a spectacular display of starlight.

The moon, full two days ago, began to rise over an outcropping at the horizon. The crickets made a quiet chirping sound, the prairie wind blew the tumbleweed, making low scratchy sounds as it scraped against his tent. The desert was as cold at night as it was hot in day. Gustave

looked out the front of his tent. His feet were down where the tent sloped to the ground. He snuggled in his warm army blanket and drifted off to sleep.

~~~~~~

"I'll take some of that coffee now," declared the voice above him. Gustave looked up. There in the early morning glow of the misty desert sun was Bill Cody, all dressed and ready for action. He was holding a prairie chicken by its legs.

"I'll clean this bird up and we'll have ourselves a right good breakfast. I got a fire cracklin' and water a boilin'. Come on now, we're in Kansas and people get up early around here!"

Gustave was pretty much dressed. He slid his boots on and crawled out of the tent. There was a little water in his bucket so he splashed it on his crusty eyes. Bill had already plucked the chicken and cleaned it out. He was fast; even found a stick to skewer it. There were two Y shaped sticks already in the ground near the fire and he placed the skewered chicken right over the embers. After a short while the chicken began to drip, the fire flared up and created an aroma drawing Gustave over to the fire.

"You rise early, Bill."

"Got to get up early while it's still cool. Best time of the day. Chicken will be done in a few minutes. How about that coffee you offered me?"

"Coffee coming right up," and Gustave reached into his haversack for the coffee beans and his homemade grinder. It wasn't long before the rich aroma of fresh brewed coffee was wafting over the small circle of tents on the West

The Legend of the Pikesville Cave

Kansas frontier. Other campers were stirring and soon there were campfires all over the place. One of the lanky campers came over to inspect the breakfast being prepared by Bill and Gustave.

"Where did you find the chicken, Bill?"

"Out a ways but not too far from the train tracks. There was a bunch of 'em running around. I got a good shot off and bagged this plump one. Scared the rest away - but they'll be back. There was a broken feed bag sitting on the ground. Might be there right now."

"Thanks a heap, Bill. I might just do that. Smells awful good. I got a lot of riding today and I needs my morning vittles." The lanky fellow headed off to his tent and picked up his Spencer rifle. It was a repeater – one of those newfangled contraptions with bullets and powder all in a single cartridge. A few minutes later there was the sound of rapid gunfire.

"I did it with one shot from my muzzle loader," Bill said proudly. "Those damn Spencers are noisy and make a lot of smoke. I always thought they were poor army weapons 'cuz the enemy could see your smoke and take you out."

"I still have my trusty muzzle loader too, Bill." As Gustave un-pitched his tent and proudly showed the gun to his new friend. "I need to get back in practice. With my scouting and demolition, I haven't had much need for shooting. But I was a pretty good shot. I popped the corks out of three wine bottles at 300 yards on my last day of training camp back East."

"You might just be in luck. If you are that good, there might be a contest over at the fort for sharpshooters like you," Bill said as he turned the chicken on the spit. It was looking almost done and was dripping less and less as the fat had all but evaporated or burned. "When I introduce you to the Captain of the Cavalry, you could sign up for the contest. It will costs a dollar to enter, but you get all the entry fees if you win. What do you think?"

"I'll have to practice, but I was good and I can be just as good again." Gustave looked at the chicken. His mouth was watering.

"Bill, you are so good to share your chicken."

"Your coffee is a treat. We don't get fresh coffee out here very much. How's your supply?"

"I have about two pounds and I hoped I could buy some more. There is no coffee for sale in Kansas?"

"Nope, the train gets here only once a week and there's mostly farming supplies on it. The railroad seems to be encouraging farmers. I'm more keen on livestock and I see Dodge growing as a center for the cattle trade with the railroad ready to haul the Texas Longhorns back East. This little place on the prairie won't be so little in a couple of years. Those Longhorns were banned further East in Kansas because of a tick that could infect the Kansas cattle. So now this is the place the big drives will be headed. Mark my words! Now let's eat!"

The succulent chicken slid off the skewer onto a big pan that Bill pulled out of his saddle bag. He pulled out his Bowie Knife and hacked the chicken in two in a sweeping blow that went right through the breast bone. Surprisingly, it  did not spatter the juices, which flooded the pan. While hardtack was not a soft bread to soak up those juices, it was better than nothing so Gustave pulled a couple of pieces from his haversack. Bill and Gustave devoured the

The Legend of the Pikesville Cave 123

succulent meat and drank down the last of the coffee. They cleaned up the dishes and packed for the journey to Fort Dodge.

~~~~~~~

Bill was on his horse; Gustave trotting along at a quick march. His burden of the haversack was relieved by Bill's horse, but Gustave shouldered his musket like a good soldier. Bill did most of the talking since Gustave would have been quite winded if he had to talk and trot at the same time.

"General Sherman is in charge of this blasted Indian War campaign. He is just as ruthless out here as he was in his scorched earth march to the sea in the Confederate War." His famous drive from Atlanta to Savannah brought Sherman fame, favor, and the appointment as the *Commanding General of the Army* after General Grant was elected President.

General Sherman
Public Domain

Bill continued, "My biggest job so far has been to carry out the general's *exterminate the Indians* policy. This is being done by killing off the buffalo that the Indians hunt. 'Remove the buffalo and you remove the Indians,' Sherman says. He's right. Without the buffalo, the Indians can't survive. So, I kill buffalo as many others do. There is a big trade in buffalo hides and a good skinner can stack up twenty hides in a day. I've seen wagon trains headed back East with 10,000 hides. Those hides make good, strong belts for the machinery in the New England mills We have so much buffalo meat that we just leave the carcases on the prairie to rot."

124   Chapter 9 Scouting in the West

Gustave listened and was immediately sickened by the thought of the slaughter and the waste. What was he getting into? He wondered about his new friend. But his money was running low and he needed to supplement his last dollars with the pay he would be getting from scouting. He hoped that would not include shooting buffalo.

Bill pointed ahead, "Fort Dodge is just about a mile from here. We'll get there by mid-afternoon. You got the gumption to continue?"

Gustave made a gesture of agreement and they continued on the march. The hot midday sun was beating down and he wished they could stop, but he didn't want to look weak in the eyes of Bill Cody.

~~~~~~~~~

Fort Dodge loomed ahead along the bank of the Arkansas River. It was in the shape of a semicircle and was cut right into the clay bank of the river. There was no stockade or heavy entrance door, but it seemed secure from Indian attacks. There were two companies of soldiers living in clay housing with sod buildings for the officers, plus a coral of horses. It looked like some brick buildings were under construction. A windless afternoon caused a wisp of smoke to rise straight up from a fire in the center of the camp. Soldiers were milling around. As they approached, a sentry came to attention and challenged them.

"Halt. State your business."

"William Cody reporting for scouting duty," shouted Bill. "This is my friend Gustave Pikestein. He is seeking Indian

The Legend of the Pikesville Cave 125

Scout assignments. We are going to see Captain Quince."

The sentry waved them on, "Proceed to the headquarters building. You know where it is, Bill."

Bill dismounted and led his horse to the watering trough. He ground hitched his steed, removing the saddle bags, the saddle, and Gustave's haversack. He handed the haversack to Gustave, who strapped it over his shoulder. Bill placed the saddle and saddle bags on a railing and motioned to Gustave to follow him to a sod house that had a HQ sign hanging at a rakish angle. The cook was beginning to prepare the evening meal over at the fire snow more than just a wisp of smoke.

"Captain Quince is inside this hot house. I don't know how he stands the place with the confounded sun. It must be hotter than blazes in here."

They entered through the low door. "Howdy, Quince, you old son of a gun," Bill shouted to a portly man in his skivvies. He was wearing only an army cap and his trousers, held up with suspenders. "Not quite regulation uniform, Lee?" observed Bill.

"Confounded heat," replied Captain Lee Quince. "I freeze to death in the winter and swelter in the summer. Only good seasons are the spring and fall. What can I do for you today Bill? And who's your friend?"

"I came back to do some more scouting and my friend is just out of the war. He is a scout. Served in Sigel's German Division. Quite a marksman to boot."

"I suppose he is looking for scouting assignments too? Well, we have a lot of scouts right now and there is not much to scout out. The Indians are suffering because we just about wiped out their buffalo," replied Quince.

126   Chapter 9 Scouting in the West

Bill looked for a moment then said, "How about some entertainment for your troops? They must be bored out of their minds with the lack of activity."

"You always were a good entertainer, Bill. What do you have in mind?"

"How about a sharpshooting contest? We could have an entry fee of a dollar and the winner gets the pot. I'm sure your men would like to join in," suggested Bill.

"I have another idea," interjected the captain. "There's one last big herd of buffalo roaming nearby and we need to wipe it out according to General Sherman's orders. Why not have a contest to see who can bring down the largest number of buffalo in a fixed time? You would be a likely participant. I have a prize of $500 for the winner."

Bill countered "I like that idea, and maybe we could also make a day of it with the sharpshooting contest too."

"Then it's a deal," said Quince. "We'll set it up for Sunday. I'll get a platoon to round up the buffalo and drive them here. You set up the place and the rules for the sharpshooters. I have a few good shots in my company and I could make it mandatory to get a big enough pot."

~~~~~~~~

Sunday rolled around in no time. Gustave had been practicing his musket loading and shooting. He was back to his old style of three rounds a minute with pinpoint accuracy at 300 yards. It was fortunate that the fort had a good supply of ammo because he had run out of powder and Minié balls for his Springfield 1861 musket.

There were fifty signed up for the sharpshooter contest. But before that event, a buffalo hunt was scheduled. It

The Legend of the Pikesville Cave

started early that morning and was set to last for a total of eight hours. Bill mounted his horse and, with his Springfield 1863, rode to the head of the first herd. His opponent Bill Comstock had a fast shooting Henry repeater rifle. The prize was the right to use the name "Buffalo" in front of their name. So the name "Buffalo Bill" would be a legendary moniker for one of the Williams – Comstock or Cody.

Comstock chased the second herd and shot the trailing animals which scattered them over a three mile trail. All in all at the end of the eight hours, Comstock killed forty-eight buffalo.

Cody used a different strategy. He went to the front of the herd and targeted the leaders. This forced the followers to one side and gather in a circle. He was able to drop these easy targets close together. With a total of sixty-eight, Cody won the match and gained the title "Buffalo Bill."

Back at the fort, he proudly stated, "My strategy and my trusty musket, which I call *Lucretia Borgia** did the job."

The troops were very much entertained by this display of marksmanship and strategy and as the day drew to a close, they were ready for a good meal of buffalo meat, and one final entertainment.

Gustave was ready too. A set of targets were set up across the back of the fort area. Each shooter was given a target to hit at 200 yards. If they missed, they were out of the competition. Of the fifty shooters, only twenty hit their target. Of course, Gustave was dead-on the mark and was ready for the next round. It was about five in the afternoon and the summer sun was still quite high. The next part of

---

* Lucretia Borgia was a legendary beautiful, ruthless Italian noblewoman, the subject of a popular contemporary Victor Hugo play of the same name.

the competition was set up a little differently. There were three targets spaced on top of each other. Each shooter had to hit all three targets again at 200 yards. Besides hitting the target, the fastest times were also recorded.

This was where Gustave had the advantage. He hit all three of his targets in fifty seconds. He was the best. But there was still more to come. Of the five finalists who managed to hit their three targets, the next challenge was to hit three targets at 300 yards and the best time would be the grand overall winner and take home the prize of $50.

The targets were set up and each contestant stood their ground 300 yards away. Two of the shooters had repeating rifles which would give them the advantage in time. The other two had Springfield 1863's. Gustave was the only contestant with an "outmoded" weapon. The first two muzzle loaders were ready and took careful aim. They got the target perfectly, but their times were in the one to two minute range. The repeater rifle shooters fired off their slick weapons, but missed at least one of the targets. They were eliminated.

Gustave had his musket loaded for the first shot. He aligned the sights for the longer distance, took careful aim and fired. The watch was ticking as he reloaded. He rammed the Minié ball down the barrel and took aim again. The clock was still ticking. He fired and the target was hit dead center. Before the shot had even hit the second target, he had the powder and Minié ball down the barrel and was aiming at the third target. If he could hit it dead on, he thought he had the time below the other two shooters. He aimed carefully and drew a deep breath. He squeezed the trigger and the gun fired just as it had been designed to do. It was like a moment suspended in time as the Minié

The Legend of the Pikesville Cave

ball flew across the field and headed to the target. Would it hit the center of the target, and would the total time of the three shots be under the minute of the closest competitor? This reminded him of the shots fired at the blast sticks when his platoon blew up ammunition train at the battle of Pea Ridge. He had not yet let out his breath as he watched the projectile hurdle to the center of the target and heard the judge cry out, "We have a winner and the champion of this whole shootin' match! Gustave Pikestein has accomplished three perfect bull's-eyes and has done it in forty-five seconds! All at 300 yards! Now that's shooting, my friends!"

Gustave stood proudly with his faithful musket straight up by his side as the other contestants flocked around him. Even the losers shook his hand and congratulated him on this amazing feat. He had not lost his touch.

The buffalo steaks were sizzling on the grill and there was even some beer. The beer was not cold, but it was wet and quenched the thirst of the men.

"We need a saloon in Dodge," came a lament from the crowd.

"Don't worry, Zeb," came a cry from one of the cavalry men. "The first building they put up will be a saloon and with girls too! There will be a lot of cowhands passing through Dodge when the cattle drives from Texas come through here."

They ate their steaks and guzzled down the beer and then there was a gradual slowing of the busy day as the moon rose over the river.

Gustave collected his $50 in prize money and Buffalo Bill picked up his $500 for killing the most buffalo. Gustave set up his tent, but used a pole for support. His musket would have a place of honor that night. He drifted off to sleep as the coyotes howled in the distance.

Chapter 10
Having a Blast on the Railroad

Gustave woke early - even before *Buffalo Bill*, as he was now known. He took his tent down and packed the few belongings he had in his haversack. There was no activity inside the fort as the men had partied long into the night and were in no shape to get up. He wondered how the City of Dodge would treat the fort and if there would be as much lawlessness as there was in other cattle towns. He hoped that a stern sheriff or possibly a US Marshal would prevail over the influx of rowdy cowboys who would inhabit the town for a few days and then drift off. He thought, "*This peaceful prairie won't ever be the same.*"

He had said his good-byes to Bill the night before and he wanted to get started back to Dodge and the railroad terminal before the sun got too high and baked him on his walk. He had $52 in his pocket and he was twenty-two years old. Indian Scouting was not his cup of tea – or mug of coffee. He decided to head farther west and see if his blasting skills were needed. The country was young and needed a lot of infrastructure – like railroads. Railroads needed track and track needed to run through mountains and there were a lot of mountains in the West.

He shouldered his musket and began the trudge back to the Dodge railroad station. He liked walking alone on the trail. There were few if any other travelers that early in the morning. His musket was loaded just in case a hostile Indian crossed his path. *"But were the Indians really hostile?"* he thought. *"They were men just like him. And they were here long before the Europeans ever settled this vast land. Why were they being deprived of their buffalo? They had lived in peace here for a very long time, hunting the buffalo and living off the land. Now the government in Washington wanted to eliminate them by eliminating their livelihood –the buffalo. No better than those nasty kings in Europe."*

He walked in thought and soon he saw the sod hut that was Dodge. The train was at the station; he bought a ticket to a place in Colorado called Durango somewhere over the border and further west. It was a long ride and the seats were not particularly comfortable but for a ticket that cost $3 it was a lot better than walking or taking a stage coach. There were a few other passengers on board and the last car had an elegant salon for (it was rumored) the owner of the railroad.

Gustave asked the conductor, "What happens when we get to Durango? Are there any hotels, places to eat?"

"Durango is mostly a railroad town. There is one hotel and it has a place to get some grub. Why are you headed that way? I see your army musket. Not much call for scouts or buffalo hunters in Durango. If that was your calling, you should have stayed in Dodge."

"I'm not much for killing buffalo. It's too majestic an animal to be slaughtered like I saw there. They had too many scouts already. I have another skill; blasting mountains for railroad track."

The Legend of the Pikesville Cave   133

"Really? Now that's a talent Dr. Bell might have a need for," the conductor said. "Let me introduce you to him. Leave your musket here. Nobody will bother with it. Follow me."

He led Gustave through the next car toward the rear of the train. It was a bit of a challenge to step out the door and over the platform into the next car of the moving train. The conductor seemed comfortable with the swaying as he nimbly negotiated the space between the cars. Gustave was a bit leery, following with great care. He was glad he did not have his long musket to balance as he rocked back and forth.

Soon they were at the last car in the train. It was vastly different from the coaches where the passengers rode. The seating was like an elegant living room. There was a large dining table and the man who was sitting at it was smoking a pipe and reading a stack of papers. There were the remnants of a meal off to his left. He looked up as they entered. "George, now just who is *this* young man?"

"What's you name, son?" said the conductor as he looked at Gustave.

"I'm Gustave Pikestein, sir."

"Gustave Pikestein, let me introduce you to the man who will be building a new line on this railroad, Dr. William Bell. Dr. Bell, Gustave tells me he has had experience blasting mountains to make space for track."

"Well, you are just the man I'm looking for," said Dr. Bell with a gleam in his eye. "What kind of blasting powder did you use?"

"We didn't use blasting powder, sir. We used blast sticks that we made with nitroglycerine."

"Nitroglycerine! That's dangerous stuff to be working with! I'm surprised that you have lived to tell the tale."

"We made the blast sticks with the help of Army Ordinance and with a formula my good friend, Gill brought back from Sweden."

"Blast sticks?! I've been reading about something like that. Some industrialist in Sweden - Alfred Nobel - I think is his name just patented a high explosive. I wrote to the DuPont company and they are sending a case of them to Durango on the next transcontinental train."

"Alfred Nobel is Gill's Uncle. We just call him *Uncle Al.*"

Dr. Bell looked surprised, "You have used this new explosive then?"

"I guess we did before Uncle Al got his patent. I hope that does not pose a problem for him. We blew up an ammunition train with our homemade blast sticks and more constructively blasted a hard rock mountainside to make way for the railroad from New York to Pennsylvania."

"I heard tell of that rail line, but I didn't know that dynamite was used. That's the name they are giving to this new explosive, *dynamite.*"

"If we didn't use *dynamite* [Gustave used the new word] we could not have done that job. The Corps of Engineers failed with mere blasting powder. When we got in with our blast sticks, I mean dynamite, we were through in just over a week."

"Young man, you have just landed a job with the Denver & Rio Grande Railway. I think you will have a blast. Sit down here and tell me more about the explosive sticks you made and have some supper. George [he spoke to the conductor who had been listening in rapt awe] get this man some supper. He's on the payroll now."

George made a hasty move to the rear of the salon car and opened a cupboard. He pulled out a dish and some cutlery and brought it to the place where Gustave was sitting.

The Legend of the Pikesville Cave 135

"Gustave, sir, shall I fetch your musket and haversack from the coach car for you?" questioned the conductor. "I think you will be continuing this trip back here with Dr. Bell."

"Right, George. Get his things, we have a lot to discuss. Having an experienced dynamite expert will very much hasten the construction of the Silverton line. Oh, and get his supper on the plate first. He must be starving."

Gustave had never been so flattered, so honored, or so served before in his life. He ate the delicious supper of fried chicken, mashed potatoes, gravy, and fresh peas with reserved gusto.

Dr. Bell and Gustave talked well into the night and then retired into comfortable beds which were made up by George, the conductor. There were a few stops along the way to pick up wood and water for the engine. It was a long trip and in the morning, when the sun came up through the salon car's windows, there was a hearty breakfast cooking on the stove which was on the other side of a partition in the rear of the car. The train was still speeding along toward Durango.

Dr. Bell was dressed and already working on his plans for the new branch of the railroad. Silver was discovered in a location that could only be accessed by train. The ore was useless unless it could be brought to a smelter and refined. That was the purpose of the Silverton branch, which would be over forty miles long and run along the Animas River. However, there were known cliffs that were too narrow even for the three foot gauge track he had planned. This is where Gustave and the new dynamite would prove to be invaluable. Bell looked over the plans and mumbled to himself - a habit he had all his life.

136 Chapter 10 Having a Blast on the Railroad

"Sir, breakfast is ready," said George. "Your new employee is still sleeping."

"Let him sleep. He probably hasn't been in a good bed in a long time. He served for over four years in the army and those conditions are not the most comfortable. He probably slept in a pup tent in the rain, heat, and snow."

Gustave began to stir as he heard the voices. The rumbling of the train and the clickety-clack of the wheels on the rails had lulled him to sleep, especially after all the talking he had done with Dr. Bell the night before. He felt a need to get up, but the bed was so delicious. Then he smelled the rich aroma of fresh brewed coffee and bacon. This was enough to shake him out of his dream – or was it a dream? He pinched himself as his mother had taught him to make sure this was real. Ouch, it was real!

He crawled out of bed and slid on his trousers and shirt and boots. He checked his purse and sure enough there was a large number of silver coins from the shooting match. He ran his hands through his hair and felt the beard he had grown during his Dodge City excursion. It was a bit scruffy.

"Good morning, Gustave," said Dr. Bell. "Breakfast is ready. Do you like coffee?"

"I do, sir, and that smells like the best coffee I have ever inhaled."

"Pour yourself a mug. We have cold milk and sugar or honey, whichever you prefer."

"This train is sure well provisioned. How do you keep things cold?"

"We have an ice car up front, just behind the baggage car. I have a load of buffalo steaks packed away in that ice car. Those steaks came from the contest at the fort. This railroad doesn't just move passengers. We move freight.

The Legend of the Pikesville Cave

That's where the real money is in railroading. There's a hotel in Durango where the patrons want the best and we provide it for them. Ice comes from the mountains. There are caves that never thaw out and I have a team of ice men who harvest the cold stuff all year round. There's a ranch with cattle for milk and meat, just outside of Durango. In the summer we grow vegetables on a farm and we have a storage building for the root vegetables. I designed it all. You can't have a town without infrastructure, I always say. Infrastructure is not just roads and buildings; it includes the things folks need to live – like food."

"You set a great table," complimented Gustave. "This coffee is the best I have ever tasted."

"Bet you haven't had bacon and eggs in a long stretch either," George said. He placed a heaping plate of bacon and scrambled eggs in front of Gustave.

"I could get used to this," said Gustave.

~~~~~~~

The train pulled into Durango. The station was far more extensive than the whistle stop at Dodge. It had a waiting room and a ticket window and a lot of people milling around.

"Welcome to Durango," Dr. Bell said. He lifted his traveling bag from the vestibule and alighted down the steps of his car. Gustave followed with his haversack and musket. He felt refreshed and ready to tackle the world. The other passengers from the cars up front staggered down the steps and looked bleary eyed after the long journey. They wandered around and dissipated from the platform. Some entered the station in a search for food. One or two

just stood there in the blazing noon-day sun stretching their legs.

George, the conductor stood by the train and just laughed. He had seen this before. These were the prospectors who had made the journey in hopes of finding a rich claim full of gold and silver. After all, the town forty miles up the river is called Silverton (for *a ton of silver*). He thought, "*...they'll be on the next train back East. All the claims are filed and there's not as much gold as the newspaper stories had said. More silver up there than gold. Poor fools.*"

Gustave followed Dr. Bell to the main street of the town. They passed a hardware store with lots of shovels and pickaxes in the window.

"Prospectors come here to strike it rich. A few do, but most don't. They spend their money in the hardware store (which the railroad owns) and then try a bit of digging in the fields up stream, but they usually are on the next train back to their old home town," pronounced Dr. Bell.

Gustave thought for a moment and said, "Too bad for them. What gets them all so fired up and anxious to come out here looking for gold and silver?"

"It's greed, my boy," counseled Dr. Bell. "Greed drives the world and greed drives it to hell. An honest job gets

The Legend of the Pikesville Cave 139

you an honest day's pay. Those trying to strike it rich are the result of dime novel fantasies and yellow rag newspapers."

"I never thought of it that way. I'm glad I have an honest job. Thank you for hiring me," said Gustave appreciatively.

They sauntered farther down the main and *only* street in Durango. It wasn't far to the hotel.

"Let's get you a room," said Bell as they entered the lobby. There were some distinguished looking men with top hats and a number of fancy dressed women decorating the chairs and settees. "Beware of those men and ladies. They're the gamblers and, well, the ladies are not *ladies*, if you know what I mean."

Gustave had heard of *the ladies of the night* during his army days. He was always too busy to try them out and his Catholic upbringing forbade such encounters. Still, they were exciting to look at.

Dr. Bell spoke to the clerk at the front desk and motioned to Gustave to sign the register. "They get fifty cents a day here for your room, which includes breakfast. Sign the register and pay for your first week."

"That will be three dollars, Mr. Pikestein. We give a discount for week stays. Breakfast is served from six until eight each morning in the dining room over there," as the clerk pointed to a double door that was now closed. "You can also get supper there. They open at five, so you have a couple of hours to rest. Tonight's special is buffalo steaks, just brought in on the train."

Gustave chuckled to himself, knowing full well that his friend Buffalo Bill had provided the dinner special. He wondered if it would taste any different than the buffalo steak he had a few nights ago at Fort Dodge. He paid the clerk with three of his silver dollars. The jingle of the money caught the attention of the ladies and especially the men in top hats. One pussyfooted his way over and when he was close enough, extended his hand in a false friendly gesture.

"Welcome to Durango, stranger. Are you here for the riches up the canyon?"

"No, sir. I'm here to help build the railroad that will bring the riches down from *up the canyon* to here for the smelter. What has made you so prosperous?"

"Why, I just make good investments and live off my wits. Are you interested in a friendly game of poker?"

The other top hat men were listening intently for Gustave's answer.

"No, sir. I don't participate in games of chance. I'm not very good at cards, and besides, I am much more skilled in blowing things up. If you would excuse me, I'm on my way to my room and then to the store to buy some clothes for my job."

The top hat man slunk away and rejoined the ladies. He was saying something to them as Gustave headed to the stairs and began the climb to his room. The lady with whom the man in the top hat had spoken sashayed over, wiggling her hips and shoulders as she made it across the room to the staircase. She spoke in a slightly exaggerated southern drawl. "Why, you handsome young gentleman, can I help you see the sights of Durango? I know all the hidden treasures that strong men like you like to see."

Gustave was at first flattered that such a beautiful lady would come over and speak to him. But then he was brought back to reality, remembering that it was not until

The Legend of the Pikesville Cave 141

the gamblers and the *ladies of the night* heard his purse jingle with the silver dollars that they paid any heed to his presence. "I thank you, ma'am, but I need my rest today and for the next week. I have a lot of hard work to do building a railroad. Now, please excuse me."

The lady turned with a bit of destain and returned to the group of vultures in the lobby. They tried their best, but Gustave was resolute in his ways. No gambling, drinking, or whoring was his mantra. He was determined not to follow in his father's path of perdition. He rounded the landing, headed up to his room, inserted the key, went inside, and locked the door behind him. "*Wow,*" he thought, "*This is one wide open town. I had better guard my money and my person from these thieves.*" He took off his haversack and laid down on the bed. It was not as comfortable as the luxury bed in the salon car, but it was not the hard ground he had become accustomed to sleeping on for these past five years. Now, if he could just keep his resolve and protect his money and keep out of trouble with women. They *were* very tempting vixens.

After an hour of rest, Gustave picked up his purse and left the room. At the desk, he asked if there was a hotel safe to put valuables. The clerk nodded a yes and Gustave turned over $30 of his loot from the shooting contest. He had a few dollars left for shopping and supper that night. The clerk filled out a receipt and put the money in a strong box which he slid into the hotel's large wall safe that was located behind the desk. Gustave felt secure now and headed out the door to find the haberdashery. The vultures were nowhere in sight and the lobby was empty.

He headed down the street beyond the hotel and soon found a men's clothing store. He noticed it was also owned by the railroad.

142 Chapter 10 Having a Blast on the Railroad

The clerk gushed, "Welcome to the Denver and Rio Grand Exclusive Men's Clothing Store. We are here at your service. Now, what can I fit you into?"

"I need some work clothes and a suit to replace these army issued trousers and shirt. Some underwear would be good also. Can you help me?"

"We have the very finest English wool suits, silk shirts, and cool cotton underwear. You know it's hard to find cotton since the South lost the war. Their fields were decimated by those Yankees. This is cotton from Egypt and is even finer than domestic."

"I need sturdy work trousers first and shirts to match. The fancy wool suits can wait until I have earned enough to afford such luxuries."

"We have very reasonable prices. I'm sure I can outfit you for under ten dollars."

"Dr. Bell told me to mention his name and that I am the new demolition engineer on the Silverton branch."

"Well in that case, I can include the wool suit for a total of twelve dollars. Dr. Bell is one of our owners and extends an employee discount to all his friends."

Gustave seemed pleased with his notoriety and the good deal on the clothing. He tried on the work clothes and the Egyptian underwear. They were quite comfortable. The wool suit, while a bit warm for an early September day was also a comfortable fit. He paid the twelve dollars and loaded with the packages of clothing, headed back to the hotel.

Back in his room, he tried on the suit and silk shirt. He felt like a dude in this finery. Without unpacking the rest of his purchases, he headed down to the dining room for supper. As he was on the landing, he was surprised to see

The Legend of the Pikesville Cave 143

Dr. Bell enter the hotel and walk over to the dining room. He sprinted ahead and caught up with his new boss.

"Good evening Dr. Bell," he said in a respectful tone of voice. "Are you here for the fresh buffalo steaks?"

"Couldn't resist. Will you join me at my table? I'd like to buy you supper and talk more about your dynamite experience. Do you know what other types of equipment we need to bring on board to expedite the blasting."

The head waiter rushed over to Bell and his friend and seated them at a prominent table in the dining room. There were many others seated and some had already been served. The succulent aroma of grilling meat drifted over the room.

"That sure smells good," observed Gustave. "My friend Buffalo Bill would be pleased that his contribution to this meal is being appreciated by so many."

"Buffalo Bill?" questioned Bell. "Tell me more about this person."

Gustave related how he had met Bill Cody at Dodge City and had watched him kill sixty-eight buffalo and win the title of "Buffalo" to add to his name. Bell was fascinated with the tale and even more so when Gustave told of his winning the sharpshooting contest. "That's how I could afford the train ride out here, the hotel cost, and the fine clothing I'm now wearing."

"You are indeed an enterprising young man. I'm proud to know you. *And* I noticed how you rebuked the gamblers and especially how you thwarted the advances of those *ladies*. You will do well in this New West. Now let's eat. I'm starving."

The supper was pleasant and the two spoke like old friends discussing how the charges would be placed down drilled holes in the side of the mountain, and how the fuses were affixed to the dynamite, and a thousand technical details about building a three foot narrow gauge railroad along a fast moving river and across gorges on bridges that spanned hundreds of feet. Dr. Bell had his plans well thought out and now the enabling piece of the puzzle was in place. He would be able to prepare the right of way along the treacherous cliffs leading to Animas Canyon with the help of his newest employee, Gustave Pikestein.

~~~~~~~

The train with the dynamite pulled into Durango a few days later. It was the second week in September and the rails and ties had already been delivered for the first few miles of the track that lead from Durango and up to Huck Finn Pond. This was easy track to lay for the terrain was relatively flat.

The chief engineer of the new rail line, Thomas Wigglesworth had his task cut out for him after that. He was good at building bridges and laying track, but blasting with dynamite was a new venture of which Gustave was the master.

The two men at first seemed to be adversaries. Wigglesworth wanted all the credit for the job and he was a bit jealous of this upstart who had impressed Dr. Bell so much. Gustave was more willing to just do his job and let personal rivalry drop by the wayside much as he dropped the rock by the wayside that his dynamite blasted from the sides of the mountains.

In the late summer and early fall, the rails pushed ahead quickly from Huck Finn Pond. The first crossing of the Animas river over a sturdy steel bridge was accomplished

The Legend of the Pikesville Cave

with little trouble. Wigglesworth was in his glory and Gustave was just a bystander wondering what he was actually doing to earn his $60 a month salary.

There was some blasting as they approached Canyon Creek and the terrain had to be leveled all along the other smaller streams like Tank Creek and Grasshopper Creek. But this was relatively simple and could have been accomplished with old fashioned blasting powder, as, Wigglesworth incessantly reminded Gustave. But the new way was still easier for the blasting material was housed in a convenient stick rather than in bags that had to be spilled into the areas that needed to be "modified." Gustave loved to look at the writing on the dynamite sticks and think how his investment in DuPont must be appreciating if he was using so much of that company's product.

As the right of way neared the treacherous Animas Canyon, rivalries had to be put aside. Fortunately, winter came later than usual when the work began. As in all railroads, especially those that are built in inhospitable places, the previous part of the trackage must be in place to get the equipment, workers, and supplies to the next part. The supply train was able to bring the steam drill, a heavy crane car, all the dynamite they would need and even more if the rock proved harder than they had previously experienced. It was slow work and the two-hundred men had to be very careful as they inched their way along the ledge just north of the town of Rockwood. That ledge had to be made wider and that was Gustave's job. The first order of business was to hoist the steam drill above the ledge and somehow plant it solidly enough to make sure it did not topple into the gorge, taking the operators with it. Among the supplies were safety harnesses which were mandatory for every worker and supervisor.

Gustave donned his harness and attached the sturdy rope that led from the harness clasp to an anchor on the track that had already been laid and was secured firmly to the flat part of the cliff they had hollowed out the day before. Yesterday's job had been relatively easy since the amount of rock that had to be blasted was only at the leading edge of the outcropping. This huge chunk of rock was the obstacle that had to be overcome in the days, or possibly weeks ahead.

The drill was up in the air, suspended by a cable from the crane car and jockeyed into position by a crew of talented workers. While the crew had experience on the flat right-o-way, and on gentle grades, aerial acrobatics were a new chapter in their lives. Both Gustave and Wigglesworth had discussed and cho-

The Legend of the Pikesville Cave 147

reographed the placement and anchoring of the steam drill. Now they were to see if their plans would work.

"If we can get three holes drilled today, we'll have done a lot," Wigglesworth lamented. "This part of the construction is going to cost us a thousand dollars a foot."

"Let's just hope we have no injuries in this *high line* part of the road," echoed Gustave. *High line* was the name being given to the area along the ledge by the crew.

The drill began to make the first indentation into the rock. It had to be held from twisting - a natural consequence of the absence of an anchor. Multiple ropes were attached to the drill and each rope was held tightly by two workmen. The workers were literally hanging over the canyon walls trying to keep the drill steady. The cold winter wind whipped up the canyon and the drill twisted as the grip of the workers was weakened. But it did not twist completely around which would have fouled it progress. The operator who was strapped to the drill on a specially designed seat had reduced the pressure when he felt the sudden wind. The steam lines also helped stabilize the drill, but they were reinforced rubber and not capable of a strong grip. However, if they were to break, the steam would scald anyone in its wild prancing if it let loose.

"That man deserves a raise," shouted Gustave over the roar of the machinery. Wigglesworth agreed.

"I'll see to that, if he survives."

"I have an idea," suggested Gustave. "Once we get the first hole drilled, we could plant a steel rod down the hole as an anchor and attach it to the steam drill."

"Great idea, I'll get a welder to fabricate an anchor," said Wigglesworth. "If I design the anchor so it has two rods, and if there is enough distance from those holes to

148   Chapter 10 Having a Blast on the Railroad

the drill, we might be able to drill two more holes before we begin blasting. In fact we could keep leapfrogging the holes until the crane runs out of reach. Then you can slide your dynamite down the first holes leaving at least two holes for the next anchoring. What do you think?"

"Sounds good," replied Gustave. The two engineers were working as a team at last.

Snow began to fall as the first two holes were completed with much straining by the workers. The short winter day was already in the shadows of the San Juan peaks. The crane lowered the steam drill and its operator back on the ground. The operator rubbed his hands. Even though he was working with steam, the cold made his fingers stiff. The crew trudged along the track and retired to the cars at the end of the work train where there would be a hot meal and bunks. They had called it a day, but they had not made an inch of progress.

"Buffalo steaks again," complained the workmen. But they ate that same, monotonous meal because they were hungry. There were some potatoes and cold beer. But they would rather drink coffee to warm themselves up. Each of the bunk cars had a potbelly stove to keep the men warm, but the wind sucked the heat out between the cracks in the sides of the wooden cars. It was a hard life, but they were being paid three dollars a day with lodging and all meals included. Three hundred dollars a year was typical earnings in those days before inflation, so a salary of $900 a year put them in a higher class than the average American.

"I wish we could get a different main dish for the men," said Gustave. "We need to keep morale up for the final drive through this, the most difficult of the entire right of way."

The Legend of the Pikesville Cave 149

Wigglesworth agreed and pulled his blanket over his face to stay warm. The two engineers could have bunked in a more comfortable salon car with a better stove and tighter caulking in the cracks, but they opted to stay with their men. Anyway, the salon car was back in Durango.

"At least breakfast has bacon and eggs and lots of coffee," remarked Wigglesworth as he drifted off to sleep.

~~~~~~~

The next morning was even more fierce than the previous night. The cold mountain wind was tunneling through the pass and everyone was freezing. "Stoke up the stove and get this place a *little* warmer," Gustave said. The cook was bundled up in a heavy coat and working over the cook stove. The potbelly had gone out and everyone's ears were tingling.

A hardy soul pulled some kindling from the wood box and got the fire started. The bunk car began to warm up above freezing. The cook stove helped and the hot coffee was a welcome liquid down the hatch and warmed the insides as the outsides began to thaw.

"What a time to build a railroad!" complained one of the workmen.

"I don't know what the weather is going to be today," said Wigglesworth. "But I need to make a new anchor for the steam drill. It's too cold out there right now, so until we have the right equipment and the wind dies down, take the day off."

"Good plan, Tom," said Gustave. "Maybe we can do better tomorrow. After breakfast I'll suggest that we play some friendly cards. No gambling. That can lead to violence."

The card game was just an activity to pass the time while Wigglesworth and the welder and the steam drill operator worked in the shop car to fabricate a new anchor contraption. He had made a measurement of the spacing of the holes they had managed to drill the day before. The holes were exactly twenty-four inches apart and the two rods were welded with a cross brace exactly twenty-four inches apart. This was affixed at the bottom of the steam drill's operator seat. The new anchor rods would be inserted in the holes to hold the drill perfectly steady while it bored the next set of holes in the side of the mountain.

"I can't wait to try this rig out," the steam drill operator said. "I can imagine how much more stable it will be. All those ropes trying to keep me steady was not a good tangle to be in."

"Maybe tomorrow," reassured Wigglesworth.

Tomorrow came and the weather was worse than the day before. The snow fell steadily and silence descended over the camp. At least the wind had calmed down. The men were getting tired of playing cards. There was plenty of food and water was fresh from the snow.

"This reminds me of the waiting in camps during my days in the army," lamented Gustave. "My father always said the waiting was the worst part of a war. This is a kind of war of the elements. At least in military camp we could drill and practice shooting."

"That's what I want to do - drill!" said the steam drill operator in jest. There was a low chuckle from the rest of the men in response to his play on the word drill joke. Soon there were other jokes being tossed around and the tone of the waiting workmen had improved. Gustave suggested telling tall stories to break the monotony.

The Legend of the Pikesville Cave 151

"I've got a good one and it might even be true," piped up one of the Chinese workers, Hong Neok Woo. He had worked on the transcontinental and had a lot of experience in mountainous winter weather.

Hong's tall tale was as follows: "*We were working in the Donner Pass in the dead of winter and the snow was piled high around our bunk cars. We had shovels and every morning we got up and shoveled ourselves out so we could get to the latrine. I remember one tunnel in the snow that a man could walk upright, straight through to the latrine. We hoped for a snowplow engine to dig us out and one day when our supplies were running low, we heard the sound of a chugging engine coming up the grade behind us. It was struggling and the drive wheels were slipping and sliding. It's a wonder that it didn't jump the tracks. But then all of a sudden, it was there in all its glory and to our cheers. We rigged a siding and the engine pulled our bunk cars off on to it and then continued its plowing. If it wasn't for that snowplow engine I would probably be buried in that wicked Donner Pass.*"

Just then the engine blew its whistle as a warning. They heard a rumbling and all of a sudden the side of the mountain was like a sheet of solid snow. An avalanche had let loose and the snow was falling down on top of them. The car rocked on the track, but held steady after the first explosive onslaught of snow and rocks and trees that rushed by them.

"Let's see how the other cars have made out," said Wigglesworth. He went to the rear of the bunk car and checked the work car. It was still there and he was glad, for the new rig for the steam drill had been left there after it had been made. Gustave checked the front of the train and saw that the cook car and the engine were still hugging the rails. Wigglesworth continued to the rear of the work car and checked to see if the crane car was still there and was serviceable. It was there, but there was a lot of tree debris in its rigging. It might take another day to untangle the mess. He checked the top of the mountain and declared, "Well, the snow is all gone up there. We won't have to worry about causing another avalanche when we start blasting. Come on men, we won't be bored any more. There's lots of work to be done to get us ready to start laying track."

The sun had broken out from the steel gray skies of the previous days and that probably had melted the snow sufficiently to cause the avalanche and the subsequent landslide. The men donned their coats and began the slow tedious work of cleaning up the crane. The cab had to be shoveled out and once that job was done it became easier to shake the debris out of the crane itself and the cables that controlled it. By evening all the snow had been tossed down into the canyon and the track was clear.

The men returned to the warm bunk car where cookie had prepared a new type of dish for them. There was still buffalo meat in the dish, but the meat had been ground up and chopped onions were mixed in plus a small amount of eggs to make a round morsel. This was fried in fat and then some sun dried tomatoes were mixed in with the fat to make a sauce. The sauce and the meat were served over boiled strands of a wheat type invention.

Cookie introduced the concoction. "I heard of this from an Italian gent back East. He calls it spaghetti and meat balls. Thought I would make a change from the usual buffalo steaks you were complaining about. I hope you like it. It's all we got tonight!"

The Legend of the Pikesville Cave

Some of the Chinese workers looked at the noodles and remarked, "This is ancient Chinese noodle. Marco Polo imported it to Italy from China many centuries ago. We like it very much. But the meat balls are something new."

The hungry crew ate the meal in silence at first, but then burst into applause. They liked it!

The moon was nearly full and that night the clear sky allowed its brilliance to cast shadows on the small mountain enclave. The men slept well with the good, warm potbelly stove and no wind blowing through the cracks in their car.

The new drilling rig worked perfectly and soon there was a section of the ledge wide enough to begin the track laying process. The dynamite worked so much better than black powder and many of the experienced workers who had seen black powder at work on the transcontinental remarked how much faster the dynamite did the job.

The work was slow, though. Some days they made a few feet on others there was enough progress to lay two fifteen foot sections of track. After a while, the early Spring helped ease the burden of the cold nights. The work, while routine, began to give indications that the end was in sight. The ledge blasting was completed in March and the rest of the right of way to Silverton was "down hill" from there.

Chapter 10 Having a Blast on the Railroad

By early July, chief construction engineer Thomas Wigglesworth declared the new "baby railroad*" born.

* Because the track gauge was 3 feet instead of the standard 4 ft 8 and one half inches, the nickname "baby railroad" was given.

Chapter 11
Maria

Gustave looked down the street of Silverton. They had completed the forty-one miles of track through some of the roughest conditions and in some of the most precarious locations. It was amazing that he had survived on some of those narrow cliffs. He had nothing but praise for his crew and their daring escapades. He felt he had certainly earned his pay, a raise to $100 a month. Gustave felt rich with over $1000 in the bank, and was ready to move on. With a recommendation from Dr. Bell (who was more of a father to him than his own birth father in Germany) he was excited to continue blasting, making the right of way and the tunnels for railroads in his growing adopted country.

He decided to spend a few days in Silverton before heading back to Durango on "his" railroad and then back East to a job in Pennsylvania he had learned about through Dr. Bell's connections. The Pennsylvania Railroad needed a tunnel through a mountain not far from where he first had experience with railroad construction while he was on loan to The Corps of Engineers.

Silverton was even smaller than Durango, but it had its dance hall and saloons. The hotel was not as fancy as Durango's *palace*, but it was a roof over his head - and the cost was only twenty-five cents a night. As Gustave headed to the hotel, he heard the train pulling into the station with a great whistling fanfare.

156   Chapter 11 Maria

"I wonder what all this ruckus is about?" he thought as he turned his attention to the small station. A passing pedestrian saw his puzzlement and interjected, "Some government monkey-monk is visiting today."

Gustave didn't give much for government officials, but walked the few feet to the station. *"Yes,"* he thought, *"Just another official looking over the supposed riches of this town. I wonder if he'll stay long?"*

The man descended from the passenger car which was at the end of the train and away from most of the cinders and smoke produced by the engine. He turned and held his hand out to help a lovely woman about his age alight from the car. Then Gustave saw a vision of elegance and beauty as he had never experienced before. A second, younger woman gracefully stepped down from the car and onto the station platform. Gustave was smitten.

While it was the middle of July, Gustave had dressed up that morning and was looking quite dashing in his silk shirt and woolen suit. He rushed over to the gentleman. "Welcome to Silverton, sir. I'm Gustave Pikestein. I was the construction engineer on the track you just rode over." Gustave was pumping up his role in the engineering endeavor just a bit. "I trust you would like a tour of the town and I'm your man to do that."

George, the conductor, was smiling in the background. He had just been promoted to Chief Conductor of the Durango to Silverton line. "Your luggage will be delivered to the hotel, Mr. Parker. You, your wife and your daughter enjoy your stay."

"May I assist you in finding the hotel?" asked Gustave.

"I think my wife and I can do that quite well, young man. I can see it now, just down the street."

The Legend of the Pikesville Cave   157

Well then, can I escort your daughter? This is a rather rough and tumble mining town and the street is a bit muddy because of the thunder storm last night."

"Why, yes of course, please take Maud's arm if you would. I'll assist Mrs. Parker."

Gustave looked into the pretty girl's eyes. "Maud it is then. And how are you today?"

"I'm a bit dusty and thirsty. I could do with a cold drink. I don't suppose there is anything with ice in it in this Godforsaken hamlet?"

Gustave was surprised to hear such language from a young lady, but took her arm and helped her descend the station platform steps to the boardwalk that made the transit from the station to the hotel a bit less muddy than walking in the rutted street. Her dainty shoes were a bit soiled when they entered the hotel lobby and her petticoats had brown streaks where they had skirted across the muddy street as they crossed to get to the hotel.

"They should have put the hotel on the station side of the street and avoid the walk through all this mess," commented Gustave. "But Dr. Bell must have had his reasons for the placement of the buildings. He is such a meticulous man."

"Is that Dr. William Bell?" asked Mr. Parker. "I had hoped he would have been here to greet us."

"Dr. Bell is back East working on another railroad project. But I'm his right hand man and would be delighted to act on his behalf," said Gustave with great enthusiasm. "I'm heading East myself in a few days, but I can stay and

158 Chapter 11 Maria

assist you and you wife and daughter for as long as you need. What is the nature of your business?"

"I'm the new Commissioner of Indian Affairs by appointment of President Grant. This is a side trip at the end of my first Western tour. I'll be heading back East myself and of course my wife and daughter will be going too."

Maud interjected, "I can't wait to get back home. I have been cooped up in too many tents and have stayed at too many Indian reservations. I may have Indian heritage, but I'm very Europeanized."

"Maud, please calm down. Show Mr. Pikestein some respect."

Parker said apologetically to Gustave, "My young daughter is very tired and I ask that you forgive her complaining. I'm sure a rest upstairs in her room will bring her back to her old cheerful self. But it's that old problem with teenagers."

"Daddy, stop calling me a teenager. I'm almost twenty. And I can't stand my name. Maud! It sounds like MUD!"

"Maud, go up to your room and cool off. Come down when you are civilized. Sometimes you act like those savages I'm supposed to be looking after as Commissioner of Indian Affairs."

Gustave took pity on Maud and got a drink for her at the hotel's bar. "Here Maud, this is a good cooler. It's Sarsaparilla and there is a big chunk of ice in it. I think it will make you feel better and having a good rest before supper will do you a world of good."

"Why, thank you Mr. Pikestein. You are so kind," gushed Maud. She took the drink and sipped it. "I like this. It is refreshing and so nice and cold. Where ever do they get ice out here in this no man's land?"

The Legend of the Pikesville Cave

"The ice comes from mountain caves. A crew goes out every week and cuts big blocks that are brought down on a small railway. These blocks are then divided up and some go down to Durango and some stay here in Silverton."

"Mr. Pikestein, you are so well informed," replied Maud as she finished her Sarsaparilla and turned to the staircase.

"Your daughter is spirted," said Gustave to both Mr. and Mrs. Parker. "She said she has Indian heritage. Can you explain?"

Mr. Parker looked at Gustave and asked, "Have you ever heard of the Seneca Indian Tribe?"

Gustave replied, "Why, no sir. I'm new to this country. I've only been here since 1861 and I fought in the Civil War for the North. So I don't have a lot of information on American History. Especially history of the original people who lived here. All I know is that most of them are to be feared."

Ely Parker

Public Domain

"That's the common idea, and it's one of the reasons I was appointed to this commissioner post. My family goes way back to the time long before any Europeans ever set foot in this country. My tribe was originally in the western part of what is now New York State."

Gustave interrupted, "Yes, I know New York State. That's where I was first stationed and where I had my basic military training. Utica was the town. And I helped build a section of track in Pennsylvania for a train line from New York State."

"Well, Utica is many miles east of my home territory in the Buffalo area. I was fortunate. My father blended in with the European settlers and I got to attend college. I am a trained engineer with a degree from Rensselaer Polytechnic Institute. I was a general in the Union Army and very close to President Grant, who was the commander of the entire Union Army at the time. But you probably know about Grant. A great man, and one who hopes to make the friction between the Indians on these plains a little less *frictional*. That's my job. So far we have managed to reduce the number of military actions against the native people and I have always been able to write treaties.

I drafted the surrender document for Appomattox and one of my proudest moments was shaking the hand of General Lee. I'll never forget that day when I was in the presence of Grant and Lee.

"At the time of surrender, General Lee stared at me for a moment. He extended his hand and said, 'I am glad to see one real American here.' I shook his hand and said, 'We are all Americans.'"

Gustave was in awe of this great man. But he was also thinking how beautiful and spirited his daughter was. He had never met anyone like her before.

~~~~~~~

Silverton wasn't very extensive nor exciting. The Parker Family was ready to return to Durango. From there, they were booked on the transcontinental and back to Washington, DC where Mr. Parker would deliver his report to President Grant.

Gustave also had his travel set up. He had arranged for inclusion of the private salon car that belonged to the Den-

The Legend of the Pikesville Cave 161

ver and Rio Grande Rail Road in the next transcontinental train. Since Dr. Bell was already in the East, this was perfectly acceptable and considered a fringe benefit of working for and being an important employee of the railroad.

"What accommodations do you have from Durango and then on the transcontinental trip?" asked Gustave of General Parker. He now addressed him by his proper title out of respect and awe - and because he was in love with his daughter.

The general replied, "Why, we have coach seats all the way. You know government officials have to keep within a budget."

"I can make that a bit more comfortable for you. I have a private salon coach at my disposal. Let me get it configured so the ladies can have their privacy and make sure there is enough food on board for all of us," boasted Gustave.

"Why, that would be most gracious, son. We would appreciate that gesture very much," said the general.

"We leave at three this afternoon. Can you be ready?" added Gustave.

"We're ready now. This little town has very little to offer in the way of entertainment," complained the general.

The trip to Durango was in coach and got them in to the station by supper time. The connection to the transcontinental was scheduled to leave early the next morning. They would have a considerable ride to the junction and their train would have only two cars: the private salon car and a supply car with ice and food just behind a stout engine. There were three guards in the supply car and a conductor. They left at seven AM.

Gustave bade farewell to George who was staying with the Durango to Silverton line as head conductor. The two friends were sorry to say good-bye. They tried to hide their tears - men didn't cry. Maud saw this display of affection and camaraderie and when Gustave had parted and was on the train, she patted him on the back and told him it was perfectly all right to express emotions. Gustave thought she looked at him in a strange and lovely way.

The trip to the junction was somewhat interesting for the first hundred miles. The rugged scenery flashed by and there would be one water and fuel stop after about three hours of travel.

It was about ten AM when they heard the first war cries. The train was traveling at about thirty miles per hour and the Indian Warriors could hardly keep up with it on their horses. The Indians knew the engine would need water and fuel and they were ready to ambush the train near the water tank just ahead. A symbolic rain of arrows fell upon the engine and the engineer was struck in the arm by one of them. Although not mortally wounded, he was unable to continue his duties. The fireman took over. He increased the speed and the Indians fell behind in their pursuit.

The passengers in the salon car were not able to see any of this and fortunately, the conductor, Herman, was with them. He immediately closed the armored window shades and advised all to sit on the floor. There was gunfire from

The Legend of the Pikesville Cave   163

the guards in the supply car. Gustave grabbed his musket and some ammunition. General Parker had a pistol and was ready to join in the battle. There were over fifty Indians in the raiding party.

"So much for treaties," said General Parker. "I hope we can outrun them."

"Oh, the train will outrun them, but we are in need of water and fuel. They were smart to attack right at the water tank. If we come to a stop down the line because we are out of fuel and water, we'll be sitting ducks," said Gustave in a concerned tone. "The best we can hope for is to outrun them and get to Fort Dodge before we run out of our essential supplies."

The Indians were out of sight and so was the water tower. The train was speeding along, but Gustave thought that would not be for long. The reserve water and wood for stoking the fire in the engine's boiler would not hold out much longer. He was on his feet now and so were the others. They opened the shutters and saw some arrows wedged into the side of the car.

"These look like Kiowa arrows," observed General Parker. "They must be renegades. I signed a treaty with their chiefs just last week. Got it here in my valise. I sort of thought the younger braves might resort to this kind of action. Wild Turkey might be the leader. There is no reasoning with those hot heads."

The engine began to slow down. Herman, the conductor looked out the door facing the supply car and saw two of the guards motioning to him. "Got to get forward," Herman said, "You all stay here."

164   Chapter 11 Maria

Herman gingerly hopped between cars and disappeared into the supply car. Gustave grabbed his musket and ammunition. "Stay here, General Parker and hold down the fort while I see what we can do to get this train going again. I have an idea."

Gustave moved forward into the supply car as the train came coasting to a stop. He walked through the car and mounted the back of the locomotive's tender that had an empty water tank and only had a few pieces of wood for the fire.

"What's the condition of the boiler?" he shouted to the fireman.

"She's very low," was the reply.

"OK, get those guards to go back in the supply car and bring pieces of ice from the cooler. Chop them up with the bayonets on their muskets. Put them into buckets and load the ice into the boiler. Is there a direct access to the boiler from the cab?"

"Yes there is and it'll melt right fast. Its hotter than blazes in there," replied the fireman.

Gustave followed the guards back into the supply car and they set up an "ice bucket brigade" by filling buckets with chopped ice and passing it forward. The fireman put the ice into the boiler and great clouds of steam rose from the access port as the ice melted and turned to water and then to steam. The fireman closed the port quickly to conserve the steam between each deposit of the ice. Gustave chopped away at the big block of ice and the process continued for ten minutes. Then the ice was gone.

In the distance, he saw a cloud of dust as the renegade Indians led by Wild Turkey galloped toward their quarry. He could see their guns blazing as they tried to hit the stranded train. But it was too far for their repeating rifles.

The Legend of the Pikesville Cave

Gustave stood on the top of the supply car and aimed his musket for its longest reach of 500 yards. He estimated the Indians were less than half a mile away and the engine was not up to full steam yet.

"Load up some of that tumbleweed in the wood storage bin. We'll need more fuel if we expect to get to Dodge," he commanded. At the same time he aimed at the lead rider and fired. Before he could see if his first shot had hit its mark, he was loaded and took a shot at the next one. It was as if both riders were hit at the same time as they crashed to the ground from their mounts that ran wild into other Indians in the party. The raiding Indians were confused and they lost ground. But now their rifles were becoming more effective. Gustave got two more lethal shots off before jumping down into the engine's cab and giving the order to "GO!"

The engine lurched as it began to respond to the ice water steam. The mighty drive wheels spun on the track and the cars clanked as the forward motion brought the train to life. As the Indians were within rifle shot distance, the train pulled away and was up to cruising speed in what seemed to take forever.

"How much longer will we have enough steam to keep us going?" questioned Gustave.

"Maybe half an hour at forty miles per hour," replied the fireman. The engineer, who was lying prone in the engine cab nodded in agreement.

"Son, you are a quick thinker," said the injured engineer. "Using the ice to tank up the boiler was a mark of genius."

After about fifteen minutes, and a ten mile distance from the last encounter with the Indian renegades, and thinking they were out of danger, they saw a dust cloud on the horizon coming right at them.

The fireman saw it first and exclaimed, "Oh, no. Not another bunch of Injuns ahead of us??!!"

As the dust cloud approached and became more distinct, Gustave made out the fluttering image of a cavalry flag.

"We're saved!" he shouted. "It's Captain Lee Quince from Fort Dodge with his troopers. Slow the train down and conserve our water and fuel."

Soon the troop of soldiers came alongside the imperiled train, which was now down to only five miles per hour as it conserved fuel and water. Gustave was on the tender.

"Captain Quince, there's a renegade Indian band less than five miles back behind us. I hit a few of them. I'm sure your troopers can clean up what's left and get them back to their elders. We think it's Wild Turkey."

Quince shouted back, "We had heard tell of Wild Turkey's band. We were heading in the direction our scout had said he would be found. You seemed to have outrun them and caused a bit of damage too. Take it easy now. We'll finish this up. Dodge is only a few miles up the track. Good luck!"

The troopers headed down the track toward the dust cloud that was quite a distance away by now. Gustave wondered if he had hit Wild Turkey in any of his four shots. He checked the condition of the engineer who was looking pale. The arrow had grazed his arm and there was a tourniquet preventing more blood from gushing out of the wound.

"Joe will be all right, Gustave," reassured the fireman. "He has been in worse scrapes before. Out here in this wild country, you get your share of close calls. Go back and check the passengers, especially that pretty one. She's a keeper - if you know what I mean."

The Legend of the Pikesville Cave 167

Gustave climbed over the end of the tender and into the supply car. The guards were sorting out the damage and the conductor was looking at the supplies, making sure there was nothing missing or spilled. "The meat will be good enough for a meal tonight, but we'll have to toss the rest of the things that were kept with the ice when we get to Dodge. There will be more supplies when we get to the junction and get cut into the transcontinental. I have money from the railroad to continue our trip and restock, so don't worry. You'll have the luxury accommodations you expect on this train. Now get back to the salon car and let the Parker family know what has happened. By the way that was the most fantastic shooting I have ever seen, Gustave. You're a real marksman!"

Gustave threaded his way through the supply car and across the platform between cars into the salon car.

"Oh Gustave, you are all right," exclaimed Maud. "I was so worried for you up there with the fighting and gunfire." She rushed to him and embraced him tightly. He had never felt a woman so close since his mother had hugged him as a child. He hugged her back. "Maud, I thank you for your concern," he blurted out the obvious. "I'm fine."

Maud let go and General Parker came over and shook his hand. "Fine work, son. I wish I could give you a medal for that performance, but now I'm only an honorary general. Tell us the details. We were all on the floor out of harm's way when the action was happening."

"Well, sir, we used the ice from the cooler to make up for missing the water tower stop. We're running on tumbleweed instead of wood for the fire, and I think I toppled four of the leaders of the band that tried to ambush us back at the water and fuel stop. The engineer took an arrow, but

168   Chapter 11 Maria

is only going to be a bit sore where it pierced his arm. The fireman is running the train. You probably saw the cavalry head down the tracks in pursuit of the renegades. They hope to capture that band and return them to their elders. The only bad news is that items in the ice cooler are now not very cold since we used all the ice for steam water. We'll have a decent supper tonight, but will have to live on emergency rations until we get to the junction. I hope that is all right with you and your family."

"Better water for the steam engine than luxury food for us," laughed Mr. Parker. "My dears, is that your thinking?"

Mrs. Parker looked at Gustave. "This fine young man whom we have only known for his generosity has saved our lives and having hardtack and salt pork is but a small price to pay for that. I will be forever indebted to you, Gustave. If I had a son, I could only have wished for such a noble, wise, and brave boy. Thank you."

Gustave blushed. Maud seemed to echo her mother's sentiments, but she did it with a hug. "Thanks," she said with tears in her eyes. Gustave could feel her heart beating rapidly through her fancy blouse.

"Well, we'll be at Fort Dodge in a jiffy. There is lots of water from the Arkansas River and wood for the engine. We'll stay the night and set off for the junction in the morning. Let's rest up for now." Gustave motioned the three passengers to sit and enjoy the rest of the ride. Conductor Herman entered the car from the supply car and was carrying a bottle of wine. "I thought we might want to celebrate our victory over the renegades with a glass of Champagne. It's still cold, but won't stay that way for long."

He opened the bottle with a pop and a fizz, pouring expertly into four glasses.

The Legend of the Pikesville Cave 169

"Herman, get yourself a glass. You should celebrate too," said Gustave.

"Why that is most gracious of you, sir, to invite me to enjoy this fine nectar of the gods," replied Herman. They drank and laughed.

Maud spoke, "Mother, I think I like my middle name more than my first name. *Maria* has a ring to it that is far more beautiful than *Maud*. I think that from now on, I will be Maria. I hope that is agreeable? Gustave, what do you think? Do you like Maria better than Maud?"

"I like the girl no matter what her name is," replied Gustave.

Part 6

Pikesville

Chapter 12
The Tunnel

Gustave held Maria's hand and placed the gold ring on her finger. "With this ring, I thee wed." General Parker and his wife Minnie watched as their new son kissed his bride. They could not be more pleased. Despite the fact that the Parkers were Baptist and Gustave was Catholic, they were amenable to the ceremony in the Catholic Church in York Pennsylvania. Maria was happy to learn about the Catholic faith and converted months before the wedding was scheduled. During that time, Gustave was working on blasting holes in mountains and along cliffs for the railroads that were crisscrossing the prosperous, growing country. It was a country just emerging from reconstruction after the great war that had once divided it.

They had settled in Pennsylvania because of the many opportunities for railroad construction. With the discovery of oil at Titusville, there was a great need for moving that "Black Gold" commodity from the wells to the refineries where the crude oil was processed into a usable product.

Gustave was presently working on a tunnel in a location just south of York. The rock was unusually hard and the steam drills were struggling to bore into that rock to allow the dynamite to slide down the hole and then slice another layer from the edge of the mountain. This was not a particularly tall mountain. Probably more like a big hill, but the Pennsylvania Railroad wanted to go right through

174   Chapter 12 The Tunnel

it. Gustave didn't argue with the railroad. He had a good contract for his expertise in blasting with the new explosive, dynamite. He was also being paid dividends on his DuPont stock that had multiplied into 120 shares since he bought the thirty shares just after the war with some of his army pay.

But today was different. He was a married man now and his bride was radiating her beauty as they walked down the aisle of the church. Gill, who was now an ordained Lutheran minister, also gave his blessing to the happy young couple. Gill had studied in Gettysburg for four long years and had been out of the seminary for a year. Not assigned to a permanent church yet, he was an assistant to established parishes in preparation for his own church and congregation.

"Gill is my best friend, Maria. We fought in the war together and he taught me all about "Blast Sticks" before DuPont ever began making them," explained Gustave to his wife of only a few minutes.

"Since Gill is your best friend, then he is my best friend also," gushed Maria. "He will always be welcome in our home. But now we must **get** to that home where we will greet our other guests who have taken off this Tuesday for our wedding."

Gustave had built a modest house in York, not too far from the church. He had prospered after the war and invested in opportunities suggested by his employers and by Maria's father; tripled his money in the five years after the war. For a man of only twenty-seven, he was quite well off.

Most of the wedding guests had walked to the house, but the happy couple took a carriage the few short blocks from

The Legend of the Pikesville Cave   175

the church to the house. Gustave made sure the driver went as slowly as possible so that they arrived after the guests had completed their walk. It was a fabulous June day with no sight of clouds and a gentle breeze from the south that made the air tingle with excitement.

As the carriage approached the house, the crowd of well wishers offered up a rousing cheer. As the bride and groom alighted from the carriage another even louder cheer erupted over the quiet streets of York.

Gustave was first to descend from the carriage and he extended his hand to his bride. Then, light as a feather, she seemed to float from the step into his waiting arms. There was no denying the love that existed between these two.

They walked up the steps of the front sidewalk and Gustave lifted Maria into his arms and walked through the open door threshold. While they had worked together furnishing the house and making it a home, this was the first *official* entrance of the happy couple.

Neighbors pitched in and the food was out on a long table that had been set up especially for the reception. This was the spirit of the "Pennsylvania Dutch" who lived in the rich farm country of this prosperous state. Gustave and Maria felt the welcome of their neighbors and made sure they too participated in the festivities and did not just act as servers. Of course, they did.

There were toasts with apple cider that had been made the previous winter. Its potency was soon demonstrated as the dancing became more excited.

Mr. Parker lifted his glass. "To the new bride and groom, I welcome my new son and bless their lives together."

"Here, here," echoed the crowd.

176   Chapter 12 The Tunnel

"To my best friend and his wife. May they live long and prosper," toasted Gill, raising his glass high above his head. "From what I have seen and heard of Gustave's success in the rebuilding of his great adopted nation, I have no doubt of even further prosperity."

The crowd of well wishers raised their glasses even higher and echoed Gill's sentiments. Many of these well wishers were part of Gustave's crew who worked with him in his blasting business. They had traveled with him to the East when he moved from the Durango and Silverton job. Gustave Pikestein was a well regarded name in the construction business.

As the afternoon slid into evening and the food began to fade from the table, the guests made their polite good-byes and headed back to their homes or, in the case of the co-workers, to their bunk train that was just down on a siding by the York terminal. Mr. and Mrs. Parker were the last to leave as the sun was setting in the west.

"Alone at last, Mrs. Pikestein," mused Gustave as he looked upon his beautiful bride.

"Yes my sweet," responded Maria.

~~~~~~~

The next morning, when he awoke beside his wife, Gustave thought of the adventure he had experienced in the ten years he had been in the United States of America. Maria was sleeping lightly and turned over to see her husband propped up on one hand, looking lovingly into her face.

"Good morning, husband."

"Good morning, my wonderful wife."

"What are you thinking about? You have such a deep look on your face," mused Maria.

The Legend of the Pikesville Cave

"I was just thinking about my good fortune in this land of opportunity; how lucky I have been; and how beautiful you are."

He leaned down and kissed her gently with all the love he could fathom up from the depth of his soul. She kissed him back holding his head with gentle fingers. They indulged in the embrace for several minutes.

There was noise in the kitchen below. Those generous neighbors were cleaning up the dishes from the festivities of the night before. It *was* ten in the morning!

"Mrs. Pikestein, we should get up and have some breakfast."

"I could just live on love, Gustave." Maria was obviously not being realistic, but she pushed the covers off and stretched in a most alluring way. She slid off the bed and headed over to the dresser, where a bowl of water was waiting. She splashed some on her face and then combed her long hair. Her long nightgown slipped from her shoulders and she splashed more water over herself.

Gustave just looked. He knew he had the most beautiful woman ever.

At 10:30 the bride and groom entered the kitchen to see the dishes all stacked up and drying in the June heat. A breakfast of fruit and fresh bread was neatly set on the kitchen table. There was a note.

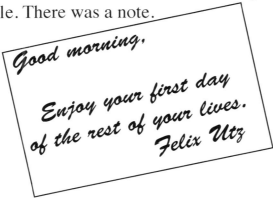

Good morning,

Enjoy your first day of the rest of your lives.

Felix Utz

"Our neighbors are so thoughtful," said Maria.

"It is wonderful to live in this part of the country." Gustave agreed and held Maria's hand. "I just wish I could have had my mother here to meet you on our wedding day. She would have loved her new daughter. That day during the war when I got the letter about her death, I cried and cried. It was the saddest day of my life. I had planned to bring her here when the war was over."

"Yes, yes, my darling. Let it out and don't ever think you can't express your feelings," consoled Maria. They had talked many times of Gustave's mother and his "lost" sister.

"But don't let me spoil today, Maria. We have each other; that's all that matters now. Let's eat this wonderful breakfast. Mr. Utz is such a gifted baker."

They spread freshly churned butter on the bread still warm from the oven and ate the strawberries that had just been picked from the garden out back. The coffee was their choice of beverage. Gustave had "converted" Maria to this potion on the cross country trip from Colorado on the transcontinental train.

"Let's clean up these few dishes and then put on our walking shoes. We will take a promenade around the town and I can show off my gorgeous wife," said Gustave.

They were a handsome couple as they strolled along the streets of York. Passers-by tipped their hats or twirled their umbrellas in acknowledgement of the newly wedded pair. They had lunch in a fashionable new restaurant on Main Street and back home, spent the afternoon just looking at each other in the most loving ways possible.

We won't interrupt this idyllic honeymoon with further descriptions. Suffice it to say, they were in Heaven.

The Legend of the Pikesville Cave 179

The next week, Gustave set off on his contracted job with the Pennsylvania Railroad. Maria was busy in her new home making curtains and beginning the plans for a warm quilt that would be a necessity for the coming winter. That would take all the rest of the summer and most of the fall to complete. She really did not want Gustave to go off to work, but she realized that their financial future depended on her husband's ability to blast holes in mountains. She wished him a safe journey and safe work. There were always dangers in the tunnel and railroad grading business.

"Now don't you worry your pretty little head off," assured Gustave, and he kissed her.

The carriage took him and his valise down the street toward the station where a special Pennsylvania steam engine was waiting with a work train consisting of a cook car, a bunk car, a work car and a crane car. The work car had the supply of dynamite that had just been shipped in from Wilmington, Delaware. It was in wooden boxes marked "EXPLOSIVES."

The train pulled out and headed south toward the mountain that needed the tunnel. As the train picked up speed, Gustave talked to his men about the hardness of the rock and asked if they had any suggestions on how to get the job done more efficiently. They offered little in the way of any helpful suggestions and it looked as if they had met a really hard place.

"Well, we'll just have to keep blasting away until we get through the east side of the mountain. We have been working on this only for a month! I may have to revise my estimated cost to the railroad," Gustave said as the train got up to full speed as it left the yard limit. They would be in the blasting zone by early afternoon and soon the drill would begin making its holes, probably in time for a few blasts before supper.

~~~~~~~

"These long summer days give us a good amount of time to get our job done," Herman, who was working the steam drill said. "But I get hungry working till sunset."

"Herman, we can blast now, so get off your drill and head into supper," countered Gustave. He slid the dynamite down the long hole in the side of the mountain. He lit the fuse and stepped away from the site. He had done this so many times it was becoming routine.

There was a rumble and much to his surprise, a huge sheet of rock fell off the side of the mountain. It was smooth on the blast side. This was unlike anything Gustave had ever seen in his seven years of making holes in rock. It was blue, not the usual red or brown rock color.

He approached the blast site and even more to his surprise

The Legend of the Pikesville Cave 181

he saw no more rock! He was looking into a vast natural cave. The final rays of sunlight sparkled on huge hanging formations of blue rock – or was it rock? From the floor of the cave there were pillars of blue rock directly below the formations that hung from the ceiling of the cave. He could hear the constant sound of dripping water and the floor of the cave was damp.

His men came to his side. "What is it, boss?"

"I don't know. I've never seen anything like this before," replied Gustave.

The last rays of sunlight dipped over the horizon and the men headed back to the train. The late supper was a buzz with speculation and wonderment about the mysterious cave and the blue pillars.

"I wonder if the light was playing tricks on us. The pillars and the inside of the cave might turn out to be just ordinary rock in the morning," was the speculation from one of the men at the supper table.

"I don't think so," replied Gustave. "I touched one of the pillars that was growing up from the floor. It felt strange; like no other rock I have ever touched. The water that was running down over its smooth surface tasted bitter and it had a bad smell."

"Yes, I thought it smelled like sulphur," interjected another workman.

The talking and speculation went well into the night but exhaustion finally claimed the men and they fell into their bunks. Gustave could not get to sleep. However, soon, just due to the long day, he nodded off. There was a lot of snoring in the bunk car. Gustave missed Maria.

182   Chapter 12 The Tunnel

Gustave's Dream

The morning broke with a faint ray of sunshine that trick-led into the vast cave. The workmen had cleared the rubble from the entrance and they now had a clear path to the interior. Because the opening was facing due east, there was plenty of light to explore. The water had puddled up in low spots and they avoided walking through them. "Boss, how high do you think this cave is?" Gustave looked up and using one of his men as a measuring stick reference, he gauged his fingers and counted, "One, two, three, four, ...eighteen, nineteen, twenty. I would say it is about twenty Herman's tall. And Herman is six feet, so it's about 120 feet high."

Gustave kept on walking and after about twenty minutes they hit a wall. It too was blue, but the light was not as bright as it was at the entrance and it was hard to tell if this was really blue.

He looked off to the side and saw another, lower cavern with more of the strange blue rock pillars. Exploring caves with different rock formations was a new idea. What if he opened this smaller portion of the tunnel to tourists. He could charge a dollar to guide them through the wondrous formations. Maybe even give the rocks names!
Just then there was a rumble and a crash.

~~~~~~~

"Boss, wake up," Herman was shaking Gustave. "There has been a cave-in or something in the cave." The rumble in his dream was real.

"Get some lanterns," ordered Gustave as he slid on his boots and stood up. The men lit the coal miners' lanterns

The Legend of the Pikesville Cave   183

and they headed down the tracks to the hole in the side of the mountain.

They saw the source of the noise. One of the pillars at the very edge of the blast site had fallen to the ground. It had probably been dislodged by the dynamite and only now had lost its grip to the ceiling.

"Nothing to worry about," observed Gustave. "But we need to be careful of those pillars. Let's get back to the bunk car and get some sleep."

The next morning was just like Gustave's dream. The sun penetrated the entrance and reached far into the mountain. "Let's be careful around the entrance. There may be more loose pillars that could fall," Gustave cautioned as they approached the opening they had blasted the evening before. They had lanterns to illuminate the way as they walked farther into the vast cave. It was just about as high inside as Gustave had reckoned in his dream. Maybe a hundred feet in places. As the sunlight faded, the lanterns picked up the interior and it remained just as blue as at the entrance. There was water on the floor and it had accumulated in puddles, which they avoided.

After a walk of nearly half an hour, they began to see the end of the cavern. The pillars had begun to get smaller when they were about halfway into the cave.

"We can lay track up to here and finish the exit from the inside. This job is going to take even less time than I had anticipated," Gustave said joyously. "Let's get back to camp and start right away."

They retraced their steps and the rest of the day was spent cleaning up the entrance where the slab had peeled away from the side of the mountain and the pillar had fallen to the floor. The crane car was especially useful in moving the slab. Rails and ties were unloaded from the work car and the track gang began laying the first of the right of way just before sunset. Supper that night was not as animated as the night before, but there was a lot of talk. Everyone slept well and the following morning, despite the rain that had begun in the early morning hours all, the men were doing their jobs and a long section of track was nearly halfway into the cave by noon. After dinner, they continued and by supper time, the track was all the way to the end of the cavern. The work train entered the cave. That night inside the cave and the interior of the bunk car, the men heard the dripping intensify. It was almost like a rain storm inside the mountain.

"The mountain must leak," thought Gustave. "That rain yesterday morning must have just made it through the ground up overhead. That must be the source of the water and how the pillars on the floor of the cave were formed. The water must dissolve the rock and the drips from the overhead pillars make the floor pillars."

The steam drill was ready and it bored horizontal holes into the rock wall. Gustave loaded the sticks of dynamite into these holes just as he would have armed his musket with a Minié ball.

The fuse was lit and the crew took shelter behind the engine which had pulled the train clear of what they believed would be the blast zone. The fuses set off their detonators and the side of the mountain blew out toward the west.

The Legend of the Pikesville Cave

They could see daylight once the dust settled. Unlike the opening at the entrance, this blast made small fragments and not the slab that had been dislodged three days before. Gustave noted, "I used a horizontal placement of the dynamite to make the smaller rock fragments. I figured that the crane car would not be as maneuverable in the cave as it was at the entrance. And, we get a lot of stone for ballast out of this. Not bad for a day's work!"

There was a little more blasting to level off the floor of the exit and by nightfall the tunnel was ready to have the last of the track laid, which was done the next morning. The track from the west end of the right–of–way was only a few hundred feet from the new track that emerged from the tunnel–cave. The foreman on that part of the line was not sure where the tunnel would have its exit, so he had not advanced his part of the track too far. Both track gangs worked over the newly surveyed right-of-way and by noon, the "Golden Spike" was driven to complete the job.

"No sense sticking around here," advised Gustave. "We'll just head back to York and I'll pay you all off. Then I can see my wife and you can go home to your families, too. Maybe a bit of summer vacation?"

The train got into York just about supper time. Gustave had missed getting to the bank, since it closed at three. He promised to go to the bank first thing in the morning and get the pay he owed his men and if they came by his house at 11, he would pay them, including the bonus. They had worked for just five weeks and the contract of $10,000 with the railroad had an expectation of completion in three months with a bonus of $2000 for each month early. Each of the twelve men got their pay for the entire three months which amounted to $300, plus the bonus of $200 for a total

186   Chapter 12 The Tunnel

of $500. Gustave withdrew $6,000 from the bank which had held the contract sum of $10,000 in escrow. He had to show the completion of the job, which he did with a document signed by the Pennsylvania Railroad supervisor who had come to see the wondrous cave that was now a tunnel. He also authorized the extra $4,000. Gustave did a quick mental calculation and realized he had amassed a fortune of nearly $7,000 after his expenses for dynamite and rental of the work train.

Gustave had paid the twelve men their well earned wages and bonuses. "If I ever do this blasting again, I'll be sure to have you with me," he said as he paid them with the new paper money issued by the treasury in Washington. The twelve piles of bills were stacked on the dining room table in his house.

Maria was astounded at the riches she saw in her house, not realizing that the bank had more than this in their account. When the last man was paid, she hugged Gustave and said, "You are the most wonderful husband a girl could ever have."

"Maria, I have an idea for an investment of the earnings from this contract. I'm going to build a new town."

Chapter 13
The New Town

Gustave sat down with Mr. Fitzroy of the real estate company of Fitzroy, Katchem, and Cheatem. There was a representative from the Pennsylvania Railroad (Mr. Morgan) and the local banker (Mr. Chased).

Mr. Fitzroy began, "The parcel in question is called Glen Rock. I believe you have just successfully blasted a tunnel through the small mountain that is on the south side of the parcel."

Gustave agreed, "Yes, we did quite a job on that tunnel and I was attracted to the adjoining parcel as a good spot for a small village. It's near the railroad and could be a place for the local farmers to do shopping when they bring their livestock and produce to the station for distribution

188   Chapter 13 The New Town

in the big cities. I believe the Pennsylvania Railroad owns the land."

Mr. Morgan piped in, "Yes, we have the deed to the mountain and the adjacent lands in a radius of a mile from our right of way."

"I believe the going price for that railroad land is four bits an acre," advised Mr. Fitzroy.

"True, but for development into a town, no matter how small it will be, we need seventy-five cents an acre," countered Mr. Morgan.

"But the town will bring business to the railroad, Mr Morgan," boasted Gustave. "In fact, I think my plan for a tourist attraction will bring a lot of passenger traffic to the town in the summer and fall."

"What's the attraction in that God-forsaken area? Just hills and valleys," retorted Mr. Morgan. The other men also looked startled at Gustave's statement.

Mr. Morgan did a quick mental calculation. "Tell you what, Gustave. If you can bring four packed passenger cars per day between June 1 and September 30, we'll give you the land for fifty cents an acre. Pay us the going price of seventy-five cents an acre now, and we'll refund the difference *if you can pack those trains*."

The deal was struck and Gustave now owned six square miles of countryside including a portion of the mountain. It took nearly half of his bank account, but left him with over $3,000 which was quite adequate in 1871 for setting up roads, building houses, and constructing business structures.

He rushed home to tell Maria of his dream town. "Are you sure the cave is a big enough attraction to get over 120 people to visit it each day?" Maria asked with a bit of skepticism.

The Legend of the Pikesville Cave   189

"People are curious and they are always looking for something new to see. I think with the right advertising, we can pull this off," promised Gustave. "With a dollar entrance fee, we can have a take of nearly $15,000 in one season. What better way to spend our money?"

"Gustave, I love you and I believe in you. What can I do to help?"

"Right now, just keep saying what you just said. I'll need all the encouragement I can get. I think my crew will be looking for new jobs. I'll contact them and we can get started tomorrow. I want to be ready for our first cave explorers by next May. But right now we need to build a village."

~~~~~~~

Gustave hired a surveyor and began the immediate planning of a small village. He assembled his old tunnel building crew and they began the task of making the rocky area that was nestled at the base of the mountain into flat, habitable building lots and a wide Main Street.

He wrote to his friend, Reverend Gilbert Nobel and proposed that he become the pastor of the church that was to be built at the west end of Main Street. "Just think of the Easter morning sunrise service with the sun streaming directly down Main Street and through the church door." Gustave continued in flowing prose. His command of the English language had vastly improved after his eleven years in the USA.

But there was more than just prose in the letters he sent to prospective business owners. He first spoke to his neighbor, Mr. Utz, and then followed up with a letter proposing that Utz's Bakery be established right next to the music shop. He cited the likely influx of farmers from the nearby Susquehanna Valley. With the railroad running right through the town, the farmers would be able to bring their produce and animals to the freight station and ship to the bigger cities up north. He cited the likelihood that these farmers would be hungry for the famous Utz baked goods and invited Mr. Utz to be a part of the new village. Likewise Gustave wrote letters and made personal contact with the prospective proprietor of the Music Shop, Mr. Levis. He also wrote glowing letters to a merchant he had seen in York and invited him to open the village's General Store.

In all his letters, Gustave emphasized the fact that there would be a fire house and a police station for public safety and security. The establishment of a church with a new minister was a plus with which he always ended his letter. Since most of the population in this part of the state were of German descent, having a Lutheran Church was a strong drawing card.

By the end of August, Gustave had his businesses lined up. Utz, Levis, and Hedgeadorn signed up for the bakery, the music store, and the market. Gill was more than pleased to take on the pastorship of the church and moved in with Gustave and Maria to help in the planning of the little town.

The grading of Main Street had progressed through July. Gustave's bank account was down to $2,000 after paying the men for the fine job they had done on this main thoroughfare. The next month would be devoted to digging the basements for the three businesses, the basements for the four houses, and basements for the rectory and church. The post office, the police station, and firehouse would have to wait until some revenue flowed in from the cave attrac-

The Legend of the Pikesville Cave 191

tion. Gustave was down to less than $1,000. That was soon gone as the first load of lumber arrived on the train in early September.

Reluctantly, Gustave approached the banker, Mr. Chased for a loan. In 1871, there was a boom going on and the banker was more than happy to make the loan of $5,000 at an interest rate of only 5%. Gustave promised to have the loan paid back by the next year, but the terms were for 3 years. His monthly payments were $160 and he had to rely on his dividends from his DuPont stock to keep current.

The first building to be completed was the bakery. Mr. Utz moved in with his ovens and bakery tables. He was so pleased with the building and had a big opening day sale. Everything was FREE! The event was publicized all over York County and hundreds of residents flocked to the bakery's first day. The next day when the donuts cost 5 cents each or 50 cents a dozen, the crowds were not crowds. Gustave's workers bought less than a dozen donuts and the few farmers who were lined up to sell their produce had about a dozen among themselves.

"Not a good beginning. I gave away more donuts yesterday than I sold all week," was the lament of Mr. Utz.

"Don't worry, we need to get the rest of the village up and running before you will see a *land office* business in donuts. You still make the best donuts in the entire county," encouraged Gustave.

As a part of the incentive to get the businesses established in Pikesville, Gustave had waived the first year rent on the buildings he had constructed. And yes, he had named the village after himself.

The market was finished in October and Mr. Hedgeadorn moved most of the merchandise from his York store to Pikesville on the train. In early November he was ready to open to the public. He did not have a free giveaway like Utz who was now doing a good business with the locals and not feeling as discouraged as he was in September.

Hedgeadorn ran some specials and soon the store was bustling with people who did not have to go all the way to York to get the things they needed to eat, decorate, or fix up things. It was indeed a general store. Hedgeadorn's motto was, "If we don't have it, you don't need it!"

The music store was a chance business. It was in the category of luxury. There was not a need for music as there was for baked goods, or nails or seeds. But the prosperity of 1871 was encouraging people to buy frivolous items like sheet music or instruments. Mr. Levis liked selling instruments because they were very profitable and he also got to sell lessons which *he* gave since he was a gifted musician.

By Christmas, 1871, the village was very lively and the church had its first Midnight Mass with Gill (or Reverend Nobel, as he became to be known) celebrating the ritual. Gustave and Maria attended out of respect and did not fear the wrath of the Catholic Church's dictate that Catholics must not attend Protestant ceremonies. Besides, Maria was pregnant and all the love and good will from the local people was a welcome blessing.

"Gustave, Gill is such a wonderful clergyman. I am so

glad you met him on that riverboat in Germany," said Maria with tears in her eyes as they walked down Main Street toward their new home on the corner right next to the bakery.

Chapter 14
The Magic Elixir

Winters in southern Pennsylvania were not as severe as in the more northern reaches of the United States. There was snow and cold, but not the deep snow of New England nor the snows that fell from the Great Lakes.

The caves that Gustave had discovered when blasting the tunnel for the railroad proved to be more exciting than he had anticipated. The main cavern was actually a tunnel nearly a mile long for the railroad and was massively high. But the side caves were a labyrinth of twisting, turning passages that were in some places only wide enough for a normal sized person to pass through, but then opened into dome shaped cathedrals with formations that were like the mighty pipe organs in European churches.

With nearly the last of his borrowed finances, Gustave purchased pipe and gas lights to illuminate the passages and some of the larger cathedrals. The temperature inside the cave was cool, but even in the coldest months of January and February, it never changed from the constant value of fifty-two degrees.

196 Chapter 14 The Magic Elixir

"This temperature will be a selling point for the hot summer months," noted Gustave as he rigged the lighting with two of his trusted helpers.

By April, the caves were ready and the advertising was prepared for inclusion in newspapers and magazines in the Eastern part of the United States.

"Let's see how this

Cool, Intriguing, Fantastic!

Visit Pike Caverns
For the Time of Your Life

Explore Natural Formations
Guided Tours
Easy To Get To

Trains Leave Daily from Major Cities for the Scenic Ride to Pikesville, PA

Admission to Caves Only $1

May 1 Through October 31.

advertising works," mused Gustave as he sent the copy off to various magazines and the local newspapers in the vicinity

The Legend of the Pikesville Cave

of York and other big cities in Pennsylvania. He spent the last of his loan money on the advertising. If no one showed up, he would be out of business and destitute. But he was confident that the lure of unknown would attract at least a few visitors. He waited with breathless anticipation for the opening day, May 1, 1872.

~~~~~~~

Besides spending money on lighting the cavern, Gustave had trained a number of guides. They were well versed in the language of cave exploration and had their spiels memorized. The scripts read like this:

"Follow me closely. The twists and turns in these caves are easy to get lost in. I do not want to lose any of you in this huge mountain."

"We are the first explorers to enter this subterranean Mecca."

"The temperature is always the same - year round."

"Just down this narrow passageway we will come to an opening that you will not believe!"

"If the great organist of the world could play on this gigantic stone organ, we would be hearing sounds like none ever heard before."

"Now be very careful as we step across this stream of water. The rock is very slippery."

"I'm going to turn the lights down now. Stay very silent and just listen to the dripping liquid as it continues to form more and more of the huge pillars that cling to the ceiling and rise from the floor. Imagine this cavern a million years ago when it was first begun."

"Now open your eyes as I bring the lights back up, and witness the splendor of the blue pillars that hang from the ceiling. They are called stalactites and the pillars on the floor, which are called stalagmites."

The Guides often interjected their own special words and

many became famous for the witty and scary things they said to the groups they brought through the twisty passageways.

One of the most popular scares was to feign that the group was lost and would never return to the surface. However, the guide would miraculously find the correct passage and then, to the cheers of the group lead them to the gift shop where the tourists could buy little pieces of rock or a liquid filled crystal ball with formations that clung to the top and bottom much like the pillars in the caves themselves.

Word of mouth advertising far outstripped the paid advertising in the newspapers and magazines, but Gustave continued to advertise. During the months of July and August, 1872, there were more than 200 visitors each day. The Pennsylvania Rail Road was very pleased with the large number of passengers and after the season ended,

The Legend of the Pikesville Cave 199

they returned the promised money. That, and with the cave admission fees, Gustave and Maria had a substantial nest egg for their little boy, who was born in June. They named him Guilford.

~~~~~~~

By early October, the visitors to the Pike Caverns had dwindled to only two passenger cars a day, but still there was substantial revenue coming in. Guilford (they called him Gil for short) was growing by leaps and bounds but was still a cute, cuddly, four month old baby.

"I have an idea for the last day of cave exploration," Gustave explained to Maria as she was changing Gil's diaper. "We need a big ending on October 31. It's Halloween and we can rig some spooky sounds in the caves. I can have Mr. Levis play a screechy violin hidden behind pillars and some of the guides can make ghost-like sounds to complete the effect. What do you think, Maria?"

"You will have to advertise it soon. Maybe you can even have a fireworks display on the mountain," added Maria.

"Great idea. I know where to buy fireworks at a discount and my crew is handy with explosives. I take it you are with me on this?"

"I can't wait," replied Maria as she placed Gil in his cradle.

Gustave drew up the advertisement and sent it off to the newspapers and a few weekly magazines where it would be published in time for the people to make plans. He also notified the rail road that they may need added cars and possibly a Pullman sleeper or two since the Pike Cavern event would go until the wee hours of the morning. He notified

200 Chapter 14 The Magic Elixir

Mr. Utz and Mr. Levis about the plans and showed them the advertising. They were happy to contribute since Gustave was buying the fried cakes and he would pay Mr. Levis for

Halloween Special!

**Visit Pike Caverns
For the Fright of Your Life**

**Last Explorations of 1872
Fireworks at midnight**

**Trains Leave Oct. 31 from Major
Cities for the Colorful Fall Ride to
Pikesville, PA**

**Halloween Party Admission $2
Includes Cider, Apple Bobbing
AND Famous Utz Fried Cakes**

**October 31
Limited Availability - Book Now!**

the music. He gathered his crew of workers and guides to make the plans for the big event.

The Legend of the Pikesville Cave   201

"Herman, I want you to go up to York to the fireworks factory and get a $50 display - you know, *the works*. Joe, Steve, Harris, you get some fine thread from the general store and string it up like spider webs. Make sure it is back lighted from the gas lamps, but don't get it too close to the flame. We don't want to have a frightful fire on our hands."

The crews and the guides followed the plan they had all worked on together and a wonderful script was written about the legend of the cave and about those who had discovered it long before Europeans had landed on these shores. It was their spirits that would be heard as the visitors of 1872 carefully walked in the hallowed halls of these ancients.

As the big day approached, the railroad sent reports on the number of passengers they had signed up. Gustave had set a limit of 200, but when that number had been reached by only October 15, he upped the total to a 300 limit. Many of the passengers had booked a sleeper and the railroad was working hard to find enough cars to accommodate the demand.

The hotels in York were all booked by mid October and many of the York townspeople who had never ventured down to Pikesville decided to come to the gala affair. The fireworks display was a great attraction that pulled in many of the cave explorers. And the promise of a thrilling Halloween experience plus a ride on a train through the Autumn colors attracted even the faint of heart.

By October 29, the railroad notified Gustave that they had booked all the available places and there were many more people asking if they could come along.

"I was right. People like entertainment and despite the relatively high cost of $2, they think they are getting a bar-

202   Chapter 14 The Magic Elixir

gain with the cider, friedcakes and fireworks," reasoned
Gustave. He began counting his revenue and expenses.

INCOME	300 @ $2 = $600
EXPENSES	
Fireworks	$50
Fried Cakes (600)	$30
Music	$25
Guides (12 @ $3/day)	$36
Cider (50 gallons)	$50
Apples (2 bushels)	$10
Misc.	$20
TOTAL	$221
Profit	$379

All the preparations were made and the cutoff of 300 visitors was adhered to. Gustave had reports that there were
some ticket scalpers who had bought the train ticket and
the entry fee and then sold them at twice the price to eager
patrons who did not sign up early enough!

The first train with the early morning visitors/explorers
pulled into the Pikesville Junction station at 10 AM, right
on schedule. There would be six trains arriving on the hour
up to 3 PM, each with fifty passengers, who would be ush-
ered off to the cavern entrance and assembled into groups
of twelve or thirteen with a guide for each group. The cave
tour took a total of forty-five minutes; started at five minute
intervals so the groups would not run into each other.

By the time the last group arrived, the visitors who had
come in early were lounging around the picnic grounds.
Mr. Hedgeadorn from the general store had ordered up a
large supply of sandwich meat and cheese and the bakery

The Legend of the Pikesville Cave

had a good supply of bread. Cider was the beverage of choice, but some of the more sophisticated patrons brought wine with them from home. It was a wonderfully warm late Autumn day with lots of sunshine and cool breezes. The people enjoyed their outing in the country.

As supper time approached, the enterprising Hedgeadorn revealed a roasted side of beef that had been cooking all day on a spit with juices dripping into a waiting pan. He had also stocked up on butternut squash and bushels of potatoes, which were also roasting. A brace of chickens were on another fire and were ready to carve into succulent morsels. It looked as if all the businesses in Pikesville were taking advantage of this spooky cave exploration day.

> **Super Supper Feast**
> **Beef or Chicken**
> **With**
> **Potatoes and Squash**
> **All you can eat**
> **$2.50**
> **Hedgeadorn's**
> **General Store**

Right after supper, the cavern tours began again. But this time the guides had rigged the spider webs and Mr. Levis was screeching in the echo chamber on his violin. He was also happy to have sold a lot of sheet music and a few instruments to the visitors.

Each of the twelve guides began the tour with a special Halloween speech. "Long ago, before the Europeans came to this great land and before any living soul that we know of today walked on this continent, an ancient people walked in this very cave."

Gustave had turned the gas lamps down to their lowest brightness to create a more eerie and spooky atmosphere. The violin squeaked in the distance. A cackle could be heard deep in the depths of the mountain. Then silence, as the lights flickered and went out! "Quiet, and you might

204 Chapter 14 The Magic Elixir

hear them now." There was utter silence with only the drip, drip, drip of the water from the ceiling of the cave - and then a tap, tap, tapping like some one-footed animal was hobbling from behind the group of twelve explorers. One of the ladies screamed and then there were more weird noises of a nondescript nature followed by more cackling.

Suddenly the lights came on again. "Let us continue and see if there is anything to my story." The group moved on and slithered through a narrow gap one at a time. Fake cobwebs were suspended above their heads, but high enough so that even the tallest did not bump and cause them to fall down. They entered into a wide chamber where the stone pillar organ seemed to be playing. Mr. Levis had a cello in addition to his violin and was playing it in the lowest registers to simulate an organ. The effect was indeed blood curdling. The lights slowly increased in intensity as the music swelled. Then the group moved on to the next chamber.

Five minutes after the first group had entered, another group of twelve began the special Halloween exploration. They too were frightened by the sounds and the special lighting effects. And through the night, all 300 guests got to be frightened, delighted, and enchanted by the theatrics that were pulled off without a single mishap. Gustave had planned and executed a fantastic event.

The guests exclaimed praise for the event as they emerged from the exit in the side of the mountain, where a big bonfire was illuminating the field.

The Legend of the Pikesville Cave

"This is better than any play I have ever seen."

"I'm going to tell all my friends about this!"

"A real exciting time!"

"Joe and Mary will be sorry that they sold their tickets."

"Best show in all of Pennsylvania."

"Yes, I'll say. Better than Buffalo Bill's Wild West show!"

"I've never been so frightened in all my life. But I felt safe with those wonderful guides."

When the guests came into the light of the bonfire, they saw tubs filled with apples floating in water. There were kegs of cider with Utz's fried cakes, just hot from the cooker, sitting on picnic tables. Many of them dived into the bobbing tubs and everybody had at least one fried cake and a mug of cider. As the witching hour of midnight rolled around, all 300 guests and the dozen guides sat back on the cool fall ground, some with blankets they had purchased at the General Store and some bundled up in warm coats they had wisely brought from home. Most of the cider and fried cakes were gone. There were many torches burning with low flickering flames.

Then there was a loud explosion at the top of the mountain signaling the beginning of the fireworks. Then there was a streak of light that seemed to climb to the moon. When it reached its zenith, it burst into an explosion of a million stars that twinkled and slowly fell back to earth. This was followed by two more rockets that burst into red and green showers of stars. Then there were three more rockets. The crowd cheered as more and more rockets burst into the air. Between the aerial exhibitions, there were pinwheels of smaller fireworks, and hundreds of firecrackers punctuating the night air.

Maria came out of their house holding the baby, "Gustave, Gil is scared. He's crying his little head off."

"We are reaching the grand finale," said Gustave. "Let me hold him. He'll be fine in a few minutes."

Maria handed Gil to Gustave, who cuddled the little bundle in his loving arms. "It's all right, little guy. The noisy fireworks will be over soon and you can go back to sleep." Gustave rocked Gil back and forth as the last of the mighty booms signaling the grand finale echoed in the distance. The people all cheered wildly and then picked up their blankets and the souvenirs of a memorable day and headed off to the railroad station to board their trains for their hotels in York or to settle down in the Pullman sleeper cars for the trip back home. As they passed by Gustave, who was still holding Gil, they extended their compliments to the entrepreneur who had orchestrated this fabulous day.

"Great show. I'm going to tell all my friends."

"Best two bucks I ever spent!"

"My family loved it!"

Gustave thanked each person for coming and slowly the crowd dissipated. "We'll clean up tomorrow morning," he shouted to his guides and workers.

Herman, who had set up and fired off the fireworks, came over to Gustave. "Boss, that first blast was a stick of dynamite on the top of the mountain on the east side just over the entrance to the railroad tunnel. It made quite a hole in the mountain, but did not damage the tunnel itself. I'm not sure, but I think the hole has a thick, blue liquid in it."

"We'll have to investigate that tomorrow when the sun is up," replied Gustave. "This might be another attraction for next season."

Chapter 15
The Panic of 1873

The winter of 1872-73 was unusually cold for Pennsylvania. Gustave had installed central heating, which was a newfangled invention. Its main design was a furnace in the basement that looked like an octopus with multiple pipes that were connected to various rooms in his two story home. Coal, plentiful in Pennsylvania, was the fuel, stored a large section of the basement called the 'coal bin.' Since his house was situated right on the rail line, it was not difficult to send the coal directly into the coal bin down a chute rigged into the side of the house from a hopper car of the train. At a cost of $3 a ton delivered and shoveled off, he had good heat for a lot less money and work than the houses with plain, old-fashioned wood fireplaces. Little Gil's nursery upstairs was warm and snuggly, unlike other houses with just a fireplace downstairs.

Herman was Gustave's trusted "right hand man" and was also the chief of police (and the only police officer) of Pikesville. He lived in the police station. His discovery of the viscous blue liquid on the top of the mountain had led Gustave to collect a sample and send it off to Harvard University for chemical analysis. He wanted to be sure the "Elixir" (as he called it) was safe to drink. He had filtered out the stone debris that the dynamite had infused into the liquid and hoped to get an assay by February. The lab at Harvard had written back stating that they had a large

208 Chapter 15 The Panic of 1873

backlog of work due to the fire (November 9, 1872) that had consumed a large part of downtown Boston. It would be about the end of February before any results became available. The liquid might be a good souvenir to sell to the cave explorers the next summer.

Two days before Gustave's 29th birthday, a letter arrived from Boston. It was the assay from Harvard that he had been waiting for.

Harvard University
Chemistry Department

February 15, 1873
"Blue liquid"
Received from Gustave Pikestein
November 5, 1872
Assay

H_2O	95%
$C12H22O11$*	3%
Copper	1%
CH_3COOH**	0.5%
Unknown	0.5%

Tested on lab rats and is not dangerous to animal life. Rats seemed to like it and flourished. One old rat perked up in an unusual manner.

* Sugar **Vinegar

Gustave knew what H_2O was and copper seemed straightforward, but the other chemical names had him stymied until he looked at the footnote stating they were just sugar and vinegar. He was glad to see that the liquid was not harmful since he wanted to taste it. The fact that the lab rats liked its taste made him get a small bottle of the liquid they had filled last November and pour a little into a glass. He held his nose (to its awful smell) and took a drink. "It's not that bad," he thought as he swallowed. It was sweet and sour at the same time. "I wonder what the unknown part is?" he mused.

Later that same day, he had Maria try a small amount of the blue liquid. She made a face as she smelled it, but drank a very small amount. "Not too bad once you get by the smell," she said. "Do you think we can sell it?"

"That's my intension," replied Gustave. "I think I'll call it the Miracle Cure Elixir. I'm going to have Hedgeadorn order some pint bottles. When the weather gets warmer we can bottle it up and paste a label with the Harvard analysis on it. I'll bet we can get $5 a pint."

~~~~~~~

By early April, Gustave had rigged a pipe from the small mountain pool that contained the Elixir to a spot just to the left of the cavern entrance. He set the spigot to let the liquid just drip into a sturdy barrel. He could run the flow faster, but he thought if he made it run slowly, the customers would think it was a much more rare

commodity. He set up a bench next to the barrel and put a sign on it reading "Miracle Cure Elixir $5 A Pint." He placed a dozen bottles on the bench.

The first cavern explorers arrived on May 1, which was a glorious, bright sunny day. There were quite a few for this early in the season and the guides took the eighty-nine people through the cavern with the same flourish as in the previous year. There was some skepticism about the elixir, but three bottles were sold to some older people who craved different and expensive things. They also had the money for their exotic tastes. It also seemed a lot of rich people had most of their money invested in the huge expansion of railroads that was sweeping the country.

Gustave had confidence in his guides and in Herman. He relaxed a bit and just watched the money roll in. He had a bank account in York with over $50,000 by early summer. His DuPont stock was soaring and had split more times than he could count. He now had over 200 shares, worth $20 a share. That was a huge gain on his original $300 investment of his soldiering pay.

Maria's father Mr. Parker, often came to visit with his wife and they made wonderful grandparents for little Gil, who was now a year old – beginning to walk and even began to say, "DA-DA and MA-MA"

"You know, Gustave, the railroads are booming and investment in their stock can be a wonderful opportunity," advised Mr. Parker.

"I like my DuPont stock, sir," replied Gustave. It pays a good dividend and I have been more than happy with the way the shares have multiplied since I bought it seven years ago. I'll stick to the chemical industry. I think there are just too many little railroads with no place to go these days. The

The Legend of the Pikesville Cave

big ones like the Pennsylvania that goes through my tunnel every day and brings my cave explorers here are the ones that will survive in a very competitive market."

"Well, I respect your opinion, but I'm with the Jay Cooke Bank and the wonderful railroad stocks they are supporting," countered Mr. Parker. "But enough talk about finances. You seem to be able to support my daughter in a grand style. Now, get yourself and my daughter off on that train to York. That Buffalo Bill's "Wild West" should be a treat for you. It will probably remind you of how we all met out there. And I want a night alone baby sitting my grandson! Well, not quite alone, I'll need to share him with his grandma."

Maria and Gustave boarded the train and headed up to York for the evening performance of the Wild West. He had received a special invitation from Bill Cody himself.

> Gustave,
>
> My show will be in York on the Fourth of July and I would really like to have you and your wife attend as my guests. I want to meet the woman who captured your heart and if you are up to it, I would like to see if you can still shoot like in the old days. I have a Springfield 1861 musket and the ammunition ready for you.
>
> Your Friend
> Buffalo Bill

When they arrived in York, they checked into their hotel and met Buffalo Bill and his wife, Louisa. They all had a dinner of buffalo steaks provided by the Wild West cowboys.

"Seem like old times, Gustave," said Bill. "Buffalo steaks are still the best meat in the country. Too bad the herds have dwindled so much. It's hard to find one today that has more than a dozen buffalo in it."

Maria interjected, "I feel sorry for the Western Indians. Their livelihood was stolen from them when the buffalo were decimated. Did you know that I am an Indian? My tribe is from upstate New York. My father was a famous General in the Civil War and wrote the surrender papers for the Appomattox."

Bill replied, "I would never have guessed you are a genuine native of this country, Maria. You seem to be so . so . ."

Maria interrupted, "Europeanized? Yes, I have lost all that rugged, savage, stereotype that most people think of as *Indian*. Actually I never had it in the first place. My grandfather just fit in with the settlers and brought my father up with a college degree and all the trappings of a white man."

"I fell in love with her from the first time I saw her in Silverton," piped in Gustave. "She was so elegant in a lovely dress and her parasol."

The dinner was over and Bill, the showman, had to get to his performance. "When I point to you in your special box seat, Gustave, I want you to get up and come into the center ring. I'll make the introduction and then hand you the musket. Do you still remember how to shoot?"

"How could I forget?" replied Gustave.

"Then do your darnedest," encouraged Bill. "I'll have my sidekick Tex Crocker help you out."

The Legend of the Pikesville Cave

They headed out the door of the hotel and walked down the street to the edge of town where the circus tent was set up for Buffalo Bill's Wild West. Maria and Gustave were seated in a place of honor along with the mayor of York and some city officials.

The show progressed and after about an hour a big lanky fellow came into the box and motioned to Gustave to follow him down to the sawdust covered floor where the performers were doing their thing. The last act was a stagecoach being attacked by Indians with Buffalo Bill leading a charge that sent the Indians off in the direction of an exit.

"Ladies and Gentlemen," announced Buffalo Bill as he reentered the center ring. "I now present for your astonishment the man who single-handedly drove off a renegade band of savage Indians and saved his future wife and her parents from their arrows and rifle fire. I give you the founder of Pikesville, Pennsylvania, the discoverer of the Pike Caverns and Springs, Gustave Pikestein – one of the best sharpshooters in the world."

Gustave sauntered down to the center ring and Bill handed him his musket. The target was rather easy at only a hundred yards. He loaded his musket and took aim, fired and just as always, hit that target dead center. But then he loaded again and again and each time hit the same spot so that it looked like he had missed the second and third shots. The crowd looked disappointed, but Bill rode around to the back of the target and proved that Gustave had indeed sliced the center ring exactly in the same spot three times in a row.

The crowd came to its feet and offered a tremendous roar of approval for such outstanding marksmanship. Gustave took his bow and listened to Bill.

214   Chapter 15 The Panic of 1873

"My friends, I am proud to have met this remarkable man in the real Wild West and to know that he lives today among you in this wonderful state of Pennsylvania!" The crowd cheered again as Gustave returned to his seat next to Maria. She hugged him with all the pride the wife of a famous person could bestow.

~~~~~~~

By the time Maria and Gustave returned to Pikesville the next day, The Wild West had upped stakes and was on to its next city. But the star attraction who had stolen the show was back in Pikesville running his own cavern tours and enjoying life in the country.

July and August rushed by. By early September, Gustave's personal account and business savings accounts had amassed a total of over $100,000. The cave tours were a huge success and the plans for another Halloween extravaganza were well underway.

But in early September disaster hit the financial markets. The Jay Cooke Bank failed when railroad overexpansion hit a serious setback. Gustave saw the failures of the big banks as a harbinger of other failures. Right after Jay Cooke failed, another big financial institution, Henry Clews,s bit the dust. He went up to York early in September and withdrew most of his funds, leaving only a token amount in a business account. He decided to "stuff his money in his mattress" instead of having it all lost in a bank failure.

Unfortunately, Maria's father had speculated in Jay Cooke's railroad investments and lost his fortune like many who saw an unlimited expansion of this booming transportation industry. Railroads had been one of the backbones of the economy, but construction of new lines of track began to fall from 7500 miles in 1872 to a mere 1600 miles in 1875. Thousands of businesses ceased to be and corporate profits vanished. Gustave's DuPont stock lost a great deal of value, but he still believed in that company and when the New York Stock Exchange reopened in early October of 1873, after ten days of closure. He bought even more DuPont stock amassing his holding to over 1000 shares. With regard to his father-in-law, he generously offered help. "We have a big house, and you are always welcome to come and live with us," he said.

But the house was not really big enough for Maria, Gustave, Gil, and their new baby girl, Louisa who was born on Gustave's birthday in 1874. So with building costs at an all-time low, the family began the plans for a new, larger home that would be on the outskirts of Pikesville. It was a colonial style, two story structure with six bedrooms on the second floor. This gave the Pikestein's lots of room for an even larger family. They gave their smaller house to the Parkers with the stipulation that they were always available to baby-sit the children. Since Mr. and Mrs. Parker were retired, they accepted the conditions with glee.

As the world–wide depression deepened, Gustave saw a sharp decline in the number of visitors to the cavern.

They still had a reasonable response to their advertising, but the thirty-thousand visitors of the first two years had diminished to less than a thousand for a season. It wasn't that the attraction was undesirable. It was just that with unemployment at a peak of nearly 9%, people simply did not have any extra money to spend on such "frivolous" entertainment. Still, bringing in a revenue of $2,000 per year was quite sufficient to pay the bills and keep a small crew of two to three guides employed. National average income in the 1870's was about $300 a year and the guides made much better than that for only six months of the year.

Now, the magic elixir was another story. At a selling price of $5 a pint and a cost of only a nickel for the bottle, the label, and the bottle cap, it was pure profit. The label stated what was in it and the "unknown" ingredient was the mystery that drew in the potential buyer. Having the analysis done by Harvard was, of course, the hook that caught many a buyer. Gustave himself drank a small amount each day just to prove that it was not harmful. About 10% of the cave visitors bought a pint and this added $500 to the yearly take even during the depression era.

As the panic of 1873 continued for two decades before the dawn of the 20th century, a new era in the history of the United States began, with unprecedented immigration beginning at the end of one of the worst depressions the world had experienced. Gustave's stock in DuPont was a very wise investment. With the "Great War," that company made a fortune in munitions. Gustave became one of the largest shareholders in DuPont and in 1918 he was asked to become a member of the board of directors of that great chemical company. He declined that offer since he was very happy to live in Pikesville and just be a grandfather.

The Legend of the Pikesville Cave

He had a total of twelve adorable grandchildren. Pikesville continued to flourish. The caverns had become a national attraction and the Halloween extravaganza drew more visitors than ever. His guides retired and their children took over, creating a tradition of stories and the legends.

The amazing thing was that in 1925, when Gustave was eighty-one years old, he did not look a day over thirty. He had continued to drink a few ounces of the magic elixir each day just to prove the potion was not harmful. Was it the "unknown" ingredient that made the Pikesville Spring, the legendary "fountain of youth?"

Epilog

1951 Pikesville, Pennsylvania, mountain country USA.

The Village Gazette hit the news stands precisely at 6 AM on December 18, 1951. It is just a week before Christmas and the pages are bursting with last minute shopping suggestions from the local merchants and a few larger out of town businesses. Pikesville is not a large village and lies in the shadow of a tall hill which is part of the Conewago Range in the south central part of the state. There are only four homes on its main street. Most of the "residents" live in the rural surroundings of the Susquehanna Valley and farm the rich soil. They all come to shop in Pikesville often stopping at the local bakery where the best donuts in the county are stacked up early every morning and are sold out by 10 AM.

There is also the Levis Music Store that is noted for unusual sheet music, instruments, and a large supply of vintage 78 rpm records.

At the end of Main Street is the Lutheran Church where Reverend Gilbert Nobel is the pastor. The population of the area is mostly 3rd and 4th generation German on this southerly side of the mountains which are south of York, the county seat.

The most famous feature of this area is the legendary Pikesville Caves and Spring. Gustave Pikestein lives here in the village he founded in 1871. But let's have the Pikesville Village Gazette tell the rest of this story.

Village Gazette

Vol. 51, No. 51   Pikesville, Pennsylvania   December 18, 1951

Santa On His Way To The Susquehanna Valley

The streets are covered with the first dusting of snow and our mountain is slick with that sure sign of Christmas. There have been sightings of the eight tiny Reindeer practicing their long winter flight.

The post Office has been inundated with last minute packages and they promise for all who mail by December 18 (that's today) a Christmas delivery will be assured. Letters addressed to Pennsylvania locations and mailed by December 20 will also get there by Christmas. Postmaster Beck assures that there will be the usual Christmas-time Sunday delivery as the Post Office will make this again, a Happy Holiday Season.

Santa's sled was sighted early on December 15th in a practice run.
-Photo by A. Zack Village Gazette

Pikestein's Gift

Our founding father, Gustave Pikestein will be passing out his annual Christmas gifts in the Church Hall. Be sure to come down at 7 PM on Christmas Eve to hear the Christmas Carol broadcast and stay for your gift.

Weather: US Weather Bureau York PA

December 18: Early morning snow with a high of 34. Clear tonight, low 23. Expect snow each day until Christmas with an accumulation of 6 to 12 inches. Seasonal temperatures in 20's and 30's.

Village Gazette Pikesville, Pennsylvania. Published Every Tuesday since 1900. 5 cents at news stand box. 4 cents home delivery. Registered, US Post Office.

The Legend of the Pikesville Cave 221

| Page 2 | Village Gazette | December 18, 1951 |

Editorial

Once again we are involved in a war in a foreign country. What started as a United Nations recommended cooperative effort by the Soviet Union and the USA to protect Korea from Japanese control has turned out to be a disaster. Communist North Korea with Soviet help is driving into South Korea. Recent battles are going badly for our troops who are thwarted by cold weather and poor military planning.

During this Christmas Season of peace and "good will to all men," let us pray that the conflict will come to an end soon and the principles of liberty and freedom will prevail.

Frost Heaves Disrupt Cave-Springs Road Crew Fixes Bump

A station wagon is caught on the bump along the Cave-Springs road.
    -Photo by A. Zack Village Gazette

Early season cold has caused a precipitous problem on the road down to the cave and spring. Cars have been impaled on the frost heave and a tow truck has been needed to free the undercarriage from the obstruction. The worst part is that the heave is on the upward part of the road and unsuspecting drivers are caught up before they know it.

A town crew has already been dispatched to grind the bump down and make travel safe again. Care should be taken this winter to avoid bumps and potholes that the subfreezing weather brings to this part of Pennsylvania.

Crew smooths bump along the Cave-Springs road.
    -Photo by A. Zack Village Gazette

222 Epilog

| Page 3 | Village Gazette | December 18, 1951 |

American Flyer Now available
At Crider's Toy Department, Downtown York

For Real Railroading right at home...

SEE 'EM ON TV
Big coast-to-coast show—
AMERICAN FLYER
BOYS' RAILROAD CLUB
See local paper for time, dates

American Flyer

The scale model electric trains that run on REAL 2-RAIL TRACK

If it's realism and authentic action you like— you want an American Flyer! No other electric train so truly captures the romance and adventure of railroading. Superb engineering and meticulous attention to detail make American Flyer Trains outstanding. It's almost as if a magic wand had been waved over real-life locomotives and cars, reducing them to 3/16 inch scale! Proportions and colors are perfect—and everything is there, right to the last rivet! A whole new world of fun begins on Christmas Day with an American Flyer Train. Why not pass the word to Dad, right now?

THIS BIG
EXCITING
TRAIN
BOOK
-YOURS FOR ONLY 10¢

GILBERT HALL OF SCIENCE
304 ERECTOR SQUARE, NEW HAVEN 6, CONN.

I enclose 10¢ for which send me immediately the huge 48-page Train Catalog filled with full-color pictures of AMERICAN FLYER Trains and accessories, PLUS Gilbert Erector sets, Chemistry sets, Magic sets, Tool sets and Puzzles.

NAME..
STREET..
CITY....................ZONE......STATE........
This offer good in U.S.A. only

AMERICAN FLYER TRAINS ARE MADE BY A. C. GILBERT, MAKER OF WORLD-FAMOUS ERECTOR

The Legend of the Pikesville Cave

Page 4   Village Gazette   December 18, 1951

Midnight Mass

The reverend Gilbert Nobel will lead the worship ceremonies this Christmas Eve starting at 11:30. The choir has been practicing and they are in good voice.

Since almost every resident and parishioner seem to attend, there will only be one mass the next day, Christmas and that will be at 9. This will give Rev. Nobel time to rest and for those who open presents early, time to do that and get to Church.

Reverend Nobel welcomes his parishioners to Midnight Mass.
-Photo by A. Zack Village Gazette

The New Super Market
Just Down Cave Springs Road. Lots of Parking

We Will NOT be Beat on Price or Availability
Turkeys 20-30 lb Toms 25¢ a pound
Tomatoes 3 pounds for 19¢
Bread large loaf 10¢
Milk Quart 18¢
Open Christmas Eve Until 6

224   Epilog

Page 5   Village Gazette   December 18, 1951

New Book!
The Legend of the Pikesville Cave

We who live in Pikesville all know the origin of our town and the legend behind it. The cave is a summer attraction that brings thousands of visitors here each year. The spring from which flows the Magic Elixir provides us with the revenue that keeps our town vital and prosperous.

Now, our founding father, Gustave Pikestein has written the definitive book on his adventures in the Civil War as a mercenary from Germany, his discovery of the cave and the spring, and his amazing longevity and vitality in this, his 107th year.

You can now read this story in his new book which is being offered exclusively at Levis Music Shop at 3 Main Street. Buy one for your children, so they too will know the story of their town. On sale now. Only 95 cents.

Pikesville Market and General Store
"The Original"
Don't be Fooled by Newcomers
Special Holiday Sale!
Turkey 23 cents a pound

Hamburger 50 cents a pound

Eggs 24 cents a dozen

Loaf of Bread 16 cents

Bacon 52 cents a pound

The Legend of the Pikesville Cave

Page 6	Village Gazette	December 18, 1951

<u>Television Schedule for the Week</u>
Brought to you by The General Store

		7 PM	8 PM	9 PM	10 PM
Tue.	CBS	News	Frank Sinatra	Crime/Suspense	Danger
	NBC	Kukla Fran & Ollie	Texaco Star Theater	Armstrong Theater	Amat. Hour
Wed.	CBS	News/ Perry Como	Arthur Godfrey	Strike It Rich	Fights
	NBC	Kukla Fran & Ollie	Kate Smith	Kraft TV Theater	Break Bank
Thu.	CBS	News/Stork Club	Burns and Allen	Amos & Andy	Big Town
	NBC	Kukla Fran & Ollie	You Bet Your Life	Dragnet	Martin Kane
Fri.	CBS	News/ Perry Como	I Remember Mama	Schlitz Playhouse	Hollywood
	NBC	Kukla Fran & Ollie	Quiz Kids	Aldrich Family	Fights
Sat.	CBS	Beat the Clock	The Ken Murray Show	Fay Emerson	Harness Racing
	NBC	One Man's Family	Four Star Review	Your Show of Shows	Hit Parade
Sun.	CBS	Gene Autrey	Ed Sullivan	Fred Waring	What's my line
	NBC	Chesterfield Sound Off	Colgate Comedy	Television Playhouse	Red Skelton
Mon.	CBS	News/ Perry Como	Godfrey's Talent	I Love Lucy	Studio One
	NBC	Kukla Fran & Ollie	Voice of Firestone	Lights Out	Montgomery

BUY YOUR NEW TV AT

New G-E Life-Size
EASY ON YOUR EYES

Imagine this beautiful 20 inch General Electric Television in your living room for Christmas. You can have it delivered from the General Store in time for the big Day! Only $299.95.

THE GENERAL STORE

| Page 7 | Village Gazette | December 18, 1951 |

Quo Vadis Opening December 27, 1951

Show Boat Held over

An American in Paris Held Over

Scrooge Now Playing Through The Holiday Season

Movies

American in Paris Held Over at Loews 4:30, 6:15, 8:00
Show Boat Held Over at Regent   4:00, 7:00, 10:00
Opening Quo Vadis at Loews Dec. 27 7:00, 10:00
Scrooge at RKO Palace   2:00, 4:00, 6:00
    8:00, 10:00

The Legend of the Pikesville Cave

Page 8	Village Gazette	December 18, 1951

Entertainment

Brought to you by Levis Music Shop
3 Main St.
Pikesville, PA

Record Hits

#1: It's No Sin   Eddy Howard (new)
#2: Cold,Cold Heart   Tony Bennett (7th week)

Top Radio Line-up

Tuesday Dec. 18
Straight Arrow (MBS) 5:30
X Minus 1 (NBC) 8:00
Yours Truly, Johnny Dollar (CBS) 8:00
Fibber McGee & Molly (NBC) 9:30

Wednesday Dec. 19
Lone Ranger (ABC) 7:30
Mr. Keen,Tracer of Lost Pers. (CBS) 8:00
This is Your FBI (MBS) 8:00
Bing Crosby (ABC) 9:00

Thursday Dec. 20
Straight Arrow (MBS) 5:30
Dragnet (NBC) 9:00
Whistler (CBS) 9:00

Friday Dec. 21
Lone Ranger (ABC) 7:30
Crime Classics (CBS) 8:00
Escape (CBS) 9:00
Sam Spade (NBC) 9:00
Suspense (CBS) 10:00

Saturday Dec. 22
Buster Brown Gang (ABC)11 AM

Sunday December 23
Shadow (MBS) 5:30
Edgar Bergen - Charlie McCarthy
(CBS) 8:00
Amos 'n' Andy (CBS) 9:00
Duffy's Tavern (NBC) 9:00
Sherlock Holmes (MBS) 9:00

Monday December 24
A Christmas Carole (NBC) 7:00
The Inner Sanctum (ABC) 8:00
Green Hornet (ABC) 9:00

Barrymore & Yule Carol

Lionel Barrymore, whose portrayal of Charles Dickens "Scrooge" has been radio "must" for the past 17 years is to be heard again in this famous role when "A Christmas Carol" is presented on the NBC network Monday, December 24, over WDOS at 7 PM.

Author's Notes

I have taken certain liberties with history in this work of fiction. Civil war fans will be disappointed that I have not been true to the actual happenings, but should be delighted with my interjection of Alfred Nobel's dynamite which was not patented until 2 years after the Civil War ended. I, of course, worked this into the story and the major theme of blasting and discovery of the cave by having a fictional relative (Gill) of the inventor in Sweden bring the knowledge of the invention to the war six years earlier than the patent on dynamite actually happened.

My great-grandfather (Benedict Berger) fought in the Civil War and had the same last name as the drill sergeant in my story (Berger). But my great-grandfather was a private and never a noncommissioned officer. In fact, he changed his name to Barker when his pay check was made out that way. So, because an "e" became an "a" and a "g" became a "k" that's my name today. Our family always thought of him as a "dumb Kraut."

The battle of Pea Ridge is of course (for you Civil War buffs) distorted. In actuality: "**Van Dorn** (The Confederate General) **found that his reserve artillery ammunition was with the wagon train, a six-hour march away.**" I have our heroes blowing up ammunition which was, in my story, on a railroad train near his camp and not in wagons six hours away. In any event, the ammo was not available and that rendered the Confederate guns useless and enabled Sigel to fire into the woods near the mountain which turned the tide of battle in favor of the Union. History sees this as a brilliant strategy and one of the few times such a "softening up" was used in the Civil War.

Later in my book, Gustave arrives at Dodge City, but this is a few years before the railroad ever got there and before Dodge was founded. While Fort Dodge was established in 1864, finding Buffalo Bill Cody there just after the war and engaged in a buffalo killing contest is fiction, but not far from the truth in terms of the prize money and who won - and within a few years of the actual date.

The later encounter with Buffalo Bill and the meeting with Tex Crocker is loosely factual (except the fact that Gustave Pikestein is fictional!). Tex Crocker was a friend and co-worker of my Father (Bernard J. Barker). I recall many very boring evenings spent at the Crocker house in Rochester, NY watching View Master slides projected in the dark. Tex boasted of being a part of Buffalo Bill's Wild West. Tex once got out his chaps and often would twirl his lariat for our entertainment. He gave me a lariat which I have misplaced. This was in the late 1940's when I was about 6. I would estimate that Tex was in his 80's or early 90's when I knew him. That would have made him a 30 year old when he was in Buffalo Bill's Wild West. (The word "Show" was never a part of the attraction name.)

The involvement of Gustave in the Durango and Silverton railroad is about 15 years before this railroad came into existence (1882). Again, for my story to progress, I had to move this event earlier in time.

Maria Parker, the love of his life, was in fact Maud Parker, who was actually born in 1878, but I needed her to be about Gustave's age. Ely Samuel Parker, her father, was a real person and a Native American from the New York State Seneca Tribe. He had been educated in engineering at Rensselaer Polytechnic Institute (RPI) and was the first Native American to serve as the Commissioner of Indian

Affairs. While Parker actually died in poverty due to the 1873 panic, I chose to provide him with a comfortable life in his later years by living in a house in Pikesville down the street from Gustave and Maria as they prospered.

The back East segment in Pikesville, PA is complete fiction and of course the discovery of the magic elixir as the fountain of youth is a critical piece of this fiction.

The images in the book were created in my basement where I wrote the story surrounded by my Gilbert American Flyer trains that were the inspiration and the "Stars" of some of the train pictures. There is an actual tunnel in the layout with the stalactites and stalagmites just as described in the story. From my world travels, I managed to find images that fit in with the story. The cover is from a cave in Vietnam. I also had visited a Civil War Reenactment in my hometown of Webster, NY for some of the images in that section.

I hope you have enjoyed this romp through the past and if you are sticklers for historical authenticity, I suspect that my fiction has challenged you to look up the real historical facts and expand your appreciation of American History.

About the Author

Thomas B. Barker is Professor Emeritus from the Rochester Institute of Technology. Before RIT, he was employed by Xerox as an engineer.

Tom has a number of interests and has managed to integrate many of them. Photography and imaging play a central role in his activities. He has produced, written, and directed Distance Learning courseware for the MS program in Applied Statistics at RIT. His experience with both still and video photography has made these efforts possible. For six years he conducted a movie camp for his two grandsons and their friends in Amherst, MA. The kids made over 10 movies in this camp and have progressed amazingly with this communication medium. He also conducted a movie camp for a troop of Girl Scouts in his home town.

His film "The Last Drop of Oil" was an official selection in the Greentopia Film Festival in 2012.

Tom has written five books on Experimental Design and its applications. He has also authored a two-volume Repair manual for Gilbert American Flyer electric trains, which is now in its 3rd Edition. His latest movie effort is with a documentary on the history of The A. C. Gilbert Company which depicts the invention of the Erector Set and the history of American Flyer Trains. He is considered an authority on Gilbert history. His other writing ("Newspaper Boy") is an historical biography of his days delivering newspapers. His books are available from Amazon.com and other retail outlets including Yesterday's Muse in Webster, NY.

Tom has garnered many awards including: Accolade (McQuaid HS), Who's Who in Colleges (RIT), Outstanding Teacher (RIT), Outstanding Quill Award (Pultneyville YC), AC Gilbert Award, Lifetime Achievement in Distance Learning (RIT).

This book, **_The Legend of the Pikesville Cave_** is his first work of fiction. It is inspired by his Gilbert American Flyer S Gauge train collection and the four layouts in his basement. He wrote this book surrounded by his trains, where he did all the photography and illustrations.

Tom lives in Webster, New York and has traveled all over the world with his wife Anne. They have a perfect sized Chinook motor home in which they travel throughout the USA.

He may be found at: amazon.com/author/thomasbarker
And his web site is: tombarker.net

Acknowledgements

I want to thank my friends who read the many initial drafts of the manuscript.

Catherine Hoffmann Bukauskas for her enthusiasm, careful reading, and finding many of the typos.

I appreciate the inputs of Joel Plotkin for his insights into how to begin an exciting book and to Susan Vorhand for her enthusiastic encouragement.

Thanks to Sergeant Paul Weis (retired) for his insights into military discipline, rank (although my congenial approach is still present), and how military secrets (like blast sticks) should be kept.

Jim Wallace helped me discover my ancestry and supplied many documents about my great grandfather.

Michael Milivojevich gave me a thirteen-year-old's take on the story and at the other end of the age spectrum, Don Matina, an army scout from WWII gave me glowing verbal reviews each time I saw this ninety-two-year-old at the YMCA where we both do our work-outs. Thanks also to the Webster Writers' Group, Art Mauer in particular.

For the "final" editing, I must thank my grandson, Jesse Barker Plotkin, for his corrections of my grammatical mistakes. I believe his education is far superior to mine – plus he has a passion for this kind of work. And before I turn this into a run on sentence (which he found many), I have to say as a fourteen-year-old, he has a future in book editing, if he so chooses.

I especially want to thank my wife, Anne, who offered encouragement, got to hear what Gustave was up to, and often joked about my five months of writing while "under foot" in the basement.

Other books
by Thomas B. Barker

Quality by Experimental Design (4 editions)
Published by CRC Press and Imprint of Taylor & Francis

Engineering Quality by Design - Interpreting the Taguchi Approach
Published by Taylor & Francis

The World is My Oyster, Coffee Table Photo/Travel
Published by Tom Barker Books, Photography & Films

Newspaper Boy
Published by Tom Barker Books, Photography & Films

Gilbert American Flyer S Gauge Operating and Repair Guide Volume 1 (3rd Edition)
Published by Tom Barker Books, Photography & Films

Gilbert American Flyer S Gauge Operating and Repair Guide Volume 2
Published by Tom Barker Books, Photography & Films

Planned Books in the Pikesville Series:

Gustave's Children
Gustave's Mother
Gustave's Sister

Made in the USA
Charleston, SC
10 December 2016